*Frederick Rolfe*

## AN OSSUARY OF THE NORTH LAGOON
## AND OTHER STORIES

FREDERICK WILLIAM ROLFE, a.k.a. BARON CORVO (1860–1913), was born in Cheapside, London. In 1886, he converted to Roman Catholicism. His short stories were published in various periodicals, including the *Yellow Book*. He wrote *A History of the Borgias* (1901), as well as a number of novels, the most famous of them being *Hadrian the Seventh* (1904). He died in poverty in Venice.

JASON ROLFE was born and raised in Southwestern Ontario. His work has appeared in numerous online and print venues. His first collection of short fiction, *An Inconvenient Corpse*, appeared as number 30 in Black Scat Books' Absurdist Texts and Documents Series (Black Scat Books, 2014). he regularly contributes to Black Scat Books' online journal, *Le Scat Noir*.

# An Ossuary of the North Lagoon

## and Other Stories

# FREDERICK ROLFE
## *BARON CORVO*

# An Ossuary of the North Lagoon
## and Other Stories

WITH AN INTRODUCTION BY

## JASON ROLFE

# CONTENTS

# INTRODUCTION

DURING periods of literary evolution we often find highly original works that are difficult to place in terms of theme and style. The stories collected here were written between 1897 and 1913, a period of dramatic global and artistic upheaval. They were written at the dusk of the Decadent movement, yet contain elements of a movement that would shortly define early 20th Century literature, producing such giants as James Joyce and Virginia Woolf. Penned by the tragitalented Frederick Rolfe, these stories helped to bridge the narrow gap between the aesthetic decadence of the 1890s and early 20th Century Modernism.

Given the defining qualities of Decadent literature, it would be easy to associate Rolfe and his work with that movement's later adherents. There is an intense refinement in it, both stylistically and thematically. As well, his characters are often found in leisurely pursuits rather than the earnest endeavours of the Victorian era. Consider the protagonist in 'An Ossuary of the North Lagoon,' and his leisurely cruise through the canals of Venice. The dreamlike laziness of the tale coupled with the subtle, transgressive sexuality prevalent throughout make it an excellent example of Rolfe's aestheticism. It exemplifies the Decadent's desire to explore the beauty of strange, subjective, and unique moments while at the same time epitomizing modern society's over-luxurious sophistication.

Such is the nature of literary evolution, that it is difficult to pinpoint the end of Decadence and the start of the Modernist movement. It should be noted, however, that the two movements were not entirely dissimilar. Both rejected the romantic Victorian notions of nature and being, focusing instead on the decline of civilization. The word *decadence* literally means, "Falling into an inferior condition or state; deterioration; decay." Both movements broke with traditional ways of viewing and interacting with the world around them. Rather than progress and growth, their adherents saw decay and felt a growing sense of alienation—an alienation that can be found throughout Rolfe's work.

In her 1924 essay, *Mr. Bennett and Mrs. Brown*, Virginia Woolf wrote, "On or about December 1910, human character changed." Many have adopted this date as the birth of Modernist thought in literature. In the same essay, Woolf admits the date is not definite; "But a change there was, nevertheless; and since one must be arbitrary, let us date it about the year 1910." If one looks more closely at the literary landscape, one can clearly see hints of modernism in works that predate Woolf's December. Alfred Jarry's *Ubu Roi* (1896) and Joseph Conrad's *Heart of Darkness* (1899) exemplify this. Intimations of modernist thought can be found throughout the works of

Frederick Rolfe as well. 'The Tattooed Wedding Ring' (1897) is the oldest story in this collection, yet the one that most easily can be associated with literary Modernism. In broad terms, the Modernist period was marked by unanticipated breaks with artistic tradition. Experimentation became a virtue. While 'The Tattooed Wedding Ring' maintains the more conventional structures of introduction, conflict, and resolution, it toys with language and sentence structure. The story's opening line, "I of the suggesting that weddings rings of men as well as women tattooed should be, maniac female, the blood, desire" foreshadows the high Modernism of writers such as James Joyce, or T.S. Eliot.

Individualism and self-examination are key elements of Modernist thought. To capture the introspective "self" and a growing sense of isolation, Modernist writers often wrote from the first person perspective. Rolfe frequently merged first person narration with metafictional commentary and autobiographical detail, giving his readers deeper insight into his troubled psyche. Each of these elements, from first person narration and metafictional thought to autobiographical wish-fulfilment (as Cecil Woolf has already pointed out, Rolfe is the "extraordinary 'slight Grey Man' who wreaks havoc in Edwardian Oxford")[1] can be found in 'The Armed Hands' (circa 1906).

The world in which Frederick Rolfe wrote changed dramatically during the course of his lifetime. It is this very act of evolution, however, that makes Rolfe's histor-

---

1 See *The Armed Hands and Other Stories and Pieces*, C. & A. Woolf, 1974.

ical context difficult to determine, and his contribution to the history of English literature is often overlooked as a result. Rolfe, the self-styled Baron Corvo, belonged, not to the past, nor to future literary movements. He belonged to the evolving literary themes and styles of the day. His work foreshadowed the Modernist movement that would eventually define early 20th Century literature. While it served as a precursor to that movement, his writing held to its deeply rooted Decadent themes, blending 19th Century aestheticism with 20th Century introspection in unique and highly intelligent ways.

—Jason Rolfe

# AN OSSUARY
# OF THE NORTH LAGOON

(JUNE 1913)

("νεκύων ἀμενηνὰ κάρηνα")

HAVE you ever seen serpents sliding out of the eye-holes of skulls? I do not mean in the depicted hells of ecclesiastical phantasy, like the great mosaic Doom in the basilica of Torçelo, but in actual fact. I have. It is a horrid sight, and a very solemn one.

What the Professor of Greek really wanted of me, I can only suspect. He belonged to that class of men which I (following Aristotle) call the Fusidowls, the Born Slaves, creatures absolutely incapable of performing a noble (*i.e.*, a free) act themselves or conniving at such performance on the part of others.

He was of that repugnant, flabby, carroty, freckled, mug-nosed, bristly species, toothed of Senigaglia-cheese-colour, which has no chest whatever. His conversation was hectic gabble, produced in the voice of a strangu-lated Punch, and punctuated with screams and stamps of rage in public piazzas, when he found that he had given a hooker a half-penny instead of a farthing, or when any of his numerous poses (Erastianism, for example) were gently gibbeted. Poses, I say: for the fact is that he (like all Cambridge graduates bubbling with a secret) was all pose where he was not savage. But he knew more Greek archaeology than any one else in the world. *Habet haec res panem.* And his brains were occasionally pickable.

For a month we had daily pervaded the lagoon north of Venice in my *barcheta.* So frequent were our progresses along all the main canals, as well as along the narrower ones which are not marked by piles, to Santerasmo, and Treporti, and Mazorbo, and Burano, and Torçelo, that we became an object of interest to the military authorities, and were warned not to photograph their forts. We did not want to photograph their forts. I, indeed, was making a frantic effort to finish writing *De Burgh's Delusion.* But Baicolo, my second gondogliere, the hugest, strongest, fairest Venetian *toso* you can imagine, a tiger with a simper, had commended himself to the Professor, who swore that he was the very image of the Agias of Delphi by Lysippos, and wished to have him anatomically photographed in the sun against a whited wall. If you know your lagoon, you will know that such a wall, suitably secluded for such a purpose, is hard to come by. Steamboats and motor-launches scuffle along all the main canals. The small ones are haunts of fishermen. Such walls as you find—they are generally crimson— enclose vineyards which swarm with barking brats and biting dogs. Whenever I stopped the *barcheta* and began to focus the camera, at that very moment Baicolo would murmur with horror, "Siori, here's people!" and shrink into concealment behind his cincture. And at last I got in a rage and roared, "I will not go to work in this hole-and-corner way. Let us find a proper place, and speak politely to the *Paron* of it, asking for half an hour of privacy behind his vine-yard wall." "Oh, God, no!" shrieks the Fusidowl. "Then we must go farther afield and find an abandoned ruin," was my conclusion. And I stood up in the golden blaze of the sun to survey the vast lagoon.

We were in the main canal which runs from the marsh north of Torçelo by Burano to Treporti, and very far away I espied a blinding, glittering stripe of white floating on its own reflection on the dancing blue. It seemed to be a walled island, and very much all alone. "And there is your whited wall," I proclaimed. But it was sixteen o'clock, and we had a seven-mile row back to Venice, so we deferred approach till the following day.

On four days thereafter we attempted to reach that wall. It was most elusive. Little canals (which seemed to be short cuts) were generally blind. The main canals led us round and round it. Once, when high water made one wide shining mirror of the lagoon, we boldly left the channels and tried to row direct across the shallows. Dire was the result—eight hours bogged on a mud-bank till the return of the tide, the Fusidowl a gibbering moist maniac, and my beloved Waterman Fountain Pen blubbering (despite the boasts of the advertisements) all over my beautiful manuscript. Needless to say that we quarrelled violently till we were faint. My grievance is easily explained. I wanted to do no more with those lovely late-August days than to sit in my *barcheta*, and be rowed about, and write my book, until I felt inclined to row, or bathe, or eat, or take my forty winks, and so on, again and again. The Fusidowl might surely have been content to sit by my side and revise his Greek-dialect proofs, and other-wise do as I did. Nothing need have prevented him from making as many photographs as he pleased. He knew how. Both the gondoglieri were agreeable. Both might have sat for Giambellini or Carpaccio—in fact I'll swear that Baicolo did, in a previous incarnation, as you may see any day at the Accademia di Belle Arti, if you do not believe me. But no, that fatuous Fusidowl neither knew exactly what he wanted, nor would let anybody tell him—neither would do his job himself, nor would let anybody do it for him. So, all of a sudden, my notorious patience gave way with a loud yell, and embellishments of lurid notes and queries. *Nemo nostrum solide natus est.*

Oh yes—we made it up when we got home, after he had sobbed and postured and gesticulated on my bed-room threshold for some hours of the night; and I saw him peacefully off to England by the eight o'clock train two mornings later. (Dear me, how exhausted I was with him!) We went up to the station together, in a hired *poppe* because of his baggage, just to show that there was no malice. My *barcheta* was waiting outside, with Baicolo and Caicio beaming and ready for devilry. And as soon as I had seen the last of the carroty professor, "We will go, I pray, for pleasure," I said to them meaningly, "by short way of little canals to Rio del Palazzo Eeale: for I have a certain affair at Ascension." "It goes most well," com-mented Baicolo and Caicio.

There is no speed limit in Venice, as far as I know, so long as you refrain from investing other boats. One ramps and rockets and rolls along, securely and courteously giving way to one's betters in *gondogle*, and requiring it of one's inferiors in all ships below the rank of a *barcheta*.

But nothing ever took precedence of mine with three oars, when I rowed one of them, not even the Duchess of Madrid's nigger-boy in her motor-launch *Ondarroa*.

Ongania, the bookseller at Ascension, gave me (for certain moneys) a couple of Italian Admiralty Charts of the lagoon, from Cioza in the south to Venice, and from Venice to the northern mainland. On the second, I soon found what I wanted—a way by canal to the island of the whited wall.

The tide was beginning to rise. The boys gleamed gaily when I said that we were going where we never had been before, an excursion of a day or two. "But, Sior— the nutriments and the beverages?" purred the luxury-loving and cat-like Baicolo. I replied that we would find those, and bedrooms, at Burano; and his hesitation dissolved in a large sunburst of a white-toothed, red-lipped, long greenish-blue-eyed smile, as he addressed his flexile muscles to the oar, punting out of the little rio by the "Bucintoro" balcony into the basin of San Marco. It was a perfect summer day of rich September. To paint it, you would have to begin by getting out your cobalt-pot and violently concentrating your mind on the potentialities of aurora-yellow. Everything which was not brilliant was blue, the sky a monstrous dome of turquoise, the water like a live aquamarine, the lights like bluebells and forget-me-nots and borage-blossoms sown upon living light, the shadows like sapphires and lapis-lazuli. Oh, those lovely little dark cool canals of the Canoniese, and Saint Mary the Beautiful, and the Mendicanti by Sanzanipolo, with their clean, clear, deep shade, and their flaming daring shafts of light, where vivid, vigorous, supple thews and sinews and bold, broad Venetian breasts (veiled in incredible patches and tatters and filth) drove prison-barges, and the *topi* or *tope* of fishers, and the *barche* of commerce, and the Blue-Cross barks, and the *sandoli* of artists and commercial travellers, flying (with hideous blasphemy) before my swift *barcheta*, with the red-cross pennon of St George of England and the red and gold *vessillo* of the local rowing-club, the "Bucintoro," until, by the Civil Hospital and Fassi's *squero*, we burst out on the north lagoon.

We had the current in our favour here; and we left San Michele on our right and the Murano glass-furnaces on our left, taking the open way past the Dazio and the islets of Sangiacomo-in-the-Marsh and Santamaria-of-the-Mount, rowing deliciously, sweeping along with the warm sea-scented wind and the flowing tide till we came near Mazorbo.

Here I drew in my own oar, and retired under the shade of the *tenda*, to study our course on the chart. "I desire, first, the *albergo* of Burano," I said to Baicolo. He lifted his *forcola*, shifting his oar back from it to mine; and we went on more deliberately through the limpid heat of noonday.

The main canal of Burano is but narrow, and crowded with the boats of the Buranelli: but, by dint of kindly addressing the owners of obstructions as "Nigger," and "That" (said, and received, with the suavest politeness imaginable), and, by the clever steering of Caicio on the *puppa* and much "drawing water" by Baieolo at the *prova*, we at last slid through, all unscraped, and moored at the clean little inn which called itself "Albergo di Koma."

Here we lunched on paste-and-beans, and grapes and cheese galore, with a nice little wine (bianco dolce) to please the palate of Caicio. I also arranged to dine and sleep there on our return in the evening: for I was pleased with the place and its *Paron*, and the clients seemed artistic and not very uncomely.

We set out again before the excursion steamer arrived from Venice, which brings tourists to be bored by Jesurum's lace-touts and indigenous incorrigible mendicity for an hour, and then takes them on to rush frantically, for twenty minutes, through the incomparable splendours of two basilicas, and a gigantic campanile, and museums, and a Devil's Bridge at all-but-deserted Torçelo, the Grandmother of Venice. And we rowed, in the gorgeous golden sunlight of afternoon, out away northward from Burano, along the sweeping curves of a wide and deep canal unmarked by piles, leaving Torçelo behind on our left, and tending north-eastward. Apparently we were making to pass the distant island of the whited wall also on our left; and the boys expressed anxiety. I fancy that I am the only Englishman in Venice who never, by any chance, permits his gondoglieri to dictate his course for him. The dog-like Caicio was by way of exhibiting *prepotenza*; but an eye as cold as agate and a withering wave of my chart reduced him to murmur most hurriedly, "It goes well—it goes very well—he" (meaning me) "is the master!" Anon, I sharply cried "Premi"; and we swept to the left, between sandbanks all ashine with sea-lavender and samphire, into a narrower water-way, which curved and curved till another short turn brought us into the haven where I would be, perhaps two miles beyond Torçelo.

We landed at the foot of the whited wall. It stood four-square, about a hundred and fifty metres each way, raised on a green island about two metres above high-water mark. The whited wall appeared to enclose a very dense shrubbery. We stuck two oars into the mud; moored the *barcheta* to them, by the bank, and landed to explore.

Caicio flung himself at the wall in front of us, and sprang up it, like a cat. "Sior, here, for gentility's sake, is nothing but verdure," he reported.

I called him down; and we turned to the right along the angle, further to investigate the exterior. At the top of the far end of the second wall there was a rusty iron cross set in the coping-stone, and (near it) a certain breach in the wall by which entrance might be made to the enclosure. I climbed in, followed by the boys.

The ground inside was very uneven indeed, quite hill-ocky as a matter of fact, and rising high above the out-side level almost to the height of the wall, in great long rather-irregular mounds intersected by great long rather-irregular furrows, and all dense with a riot of bushy and weedy under-growth, like a Venetian attempt at a jungle. But, in front of us as we entered, there was a mere sem-blance of thinning, an apology for the remains of an age-long neglected pathway. Ascending the first mound, I began to pace along the narrow clearing.

And, as I stepped cautiously, I was aware that the ground under me was crackling and murmuring and whispering very strangely. I glared back at my boys, who were following me: their jaws were dropped and their faces pallid. I went on. Such surface of earth as there was appeared to be loosely and thinly scattered over what I took to be fragments of faggots of very old sun-whitened sticks—sticks which occasionally had knobby ends—Gracious Powers!—brittle, or broken. Perhaps I stumbled a dozen paces up the crooked path; and then, from the summit, all of a sudden I saw the bare side of the next long irregular mound. But the surface had fallen away from it, or some storm had washed it naked. And I found myself staring, glaring, at a massed congeries of whole and broken human skeletons, male by the pelvis I judged at first glance. *And two long black serpents wriggled through the eye-holes of skulls within reach of my foot; and slid away into the bushes.*

Oh, plainly I had made an unthought-of and paralysing discovery. There was a short sharp movement in my rear.

"Pray for the repose of the souls of all these poor abandoned desolate dead. Requiem aeternam dona eis, Domine," I instantly intoned aloud.

"*Et lux perpetua luceat eis,*" Baicolo piously and automatically responded.

"O Mariavergine!" gasped Caicio.

But I had stopped them from bolting scut-up; and they hung on my heels clutching at each other's vesture.

I extended my explorations. It was impossible to go very far, not more than thirty metres, into the depth of the enclosure; because the phantom of a path, such as it was, tailed off miserably into the lush impenetrable jungle. But, wherever the eye could pierce, we saw similar rather irregular long mounds, which the slightest kick of a toe disclosed to be formed entirely of human remains in hundreds (to speak quite disparagingly). And, on all sides, hung the same awful blazing silence rustling with weird whisperings, and the same vivid sickly riot of verdure rooted in human dust.

We retraced our steps, and went along the outside of the third wall. And at its far end, also, there was a broken place, not so ruinous as the breach in the second wall, by which we made a new invasion. Here we saw more mounds, more dolorous piles on piles of skeletons, more grinning fragmentary skulls, more rain-stained, wind-dried, sun-bleached thigh-bones and shoulder-blades, than I have ever seen in all my most horrid dreams put together, chucked down at random, higgledy-piggledy, in gruesome heaps, solemnly exposed and upbraidingly appealing to the solemnly winking sky and the salt sea air and the blinding illimitable sunlight.

"What in the world is this place?" I demanded at large, as we hurriedly scrambled out, and walked along the outside of the fourth wall, with a narrow canal on our right, and the miles and miles and miles of marsh beyond it.

"Sior, mi no eo gnente de gnente—Sir, I don't know nothing about nothing," flatly declared Caicio, with no interest whatever, and true Venetian shamelessness at his much negatived and totally positive ignorance.

At the fourth angle I found another rusty iron cross like the one which I had found at the second, but lying anyhow on the ground at the foot of the wall with the coping-stone in which it had been lead-bedded. Of course I wished to replace it; but its proper site was so covered with at least twenty years' growth of wild ivy that there was nothing to be done but to fix the sacred symbol erect and fairly conspicuous on the grass where it had fallen.

We were on the whited side again—the other three were reddish-yellow—and out in the full sunlight nearing the place of our landing. Here the top of the bank was wider, as deliberately wide as a terrace; and I paced slowly along it, wondering what it really was which I had seen. Evidently the task of picking the brains of the most ancient and most contiguous autochthones was clearly indicated as mine. And then, to add to my confusion, I suddenly came upon two stone slabs embedded in the middle of the whited wall. They were of the eighteenth century, incised with armorials and inscriptions. The latter declared the enclosure of a cemetery by a four-square wall; and the former blazoned the achievements of certain Illustrissimi of the Most Serene Republic.

We got back into the *barcheta*. The boys instantly fell on sleep in the deep shade of *puppa* and *prova*. I spread out my charts under the *tenda*, and sat down to ponder my discovery.

On the chart, my island ossuary (which is unknown by all the Englishmen I ever met in Venice) is most distinctly denominated Santariano. The nearest island in sight, under a quarter of a mile to the east-north-eastward, is a vineyard with a picturesque old house and Watergate; and the chart calls it Santacristina. Evidently my island was a cemetery. The inscriptions proclaimed the fact. But what sort of a cemetery was it, in the Names of Goodness and Saint Phocas the Patron of Gravediggers? For the awful miscellaneous aggregation of piteous blasted bones (which I had seen) was in no sense interred, but heaped upon the surface of this eighteenth-century "cemetery," in monstrous, rather irregular long mounds, flung upon the level of the island, piled above it heterogeneously. And its sole shroud was not else than fortuitous atoms of decent dust, accumulated by the winds of heaven (more pitiful than man), during long long years. And the bushes and the weeds grew and flourished rankly through and through it all.

"What does an island full of bones beyond Torçelo call itself?" I asked, after dinner that night, of the fat *paron* of the Buranello *albergo*.

He summoned his *barcajuolo*, for he himself came from the Friuli, and knew nothing and wanted to know nothing of the Venetian lagoon. "Ciò, Bepi," says he, "this Sior Inglese would know what an island full of bones beyond Torçelo calls itself?"

"It calls itself, Sior, with permission, Santacristina."

"But no, but no," I howled, "Santacristina is the next island—the one with the vine-yard."

"Sissiorsì," solemnly agrees Bepi.

"And then, the island full of bones?" I demanded again.

"Also Santacristina, also that," asseverates Bepi.

I delayed the tearing of my hair, at least for the moment. No one can ever accuse me of undue precipitancy: indeed, my much more than Jobian patience and forbearance is generally taken for timidity and weakness. It was inconceivable that both islands, islands so thoroughly separate, should have the same name. And, curbing my desire to be violent, I spread out my chart and showed the two islands with their two names Santariano and Santacristina respectively. All the people in the inn, artists, writers, models, and the usual Buranelli shop-keepers, officials, fishermen, sindaco, who degusted there their modest nightly potions, crowded round my table, dully eyed my chart, and interminably discussed the portent thereon set down. But no one had ever even heard of Santariano: both islands called themselves Santacristina: my chart had mistaken itself; and my island full of bones (they might mention) was an immemorially desolate cemetery, hideously haunted by husky whisperers (*bis-bigliatori*), and an accursed spot sedulously to be avoided by all well-living Christian men. And some made horns, others the Sign of the Cross.

But I persisted, wanting to know (*per gentilezza*) whose piteous bones were heaped up there so ruthlessly. And no one would tell me. I really believe that no one could tell me, that no one had ever taken the trouble to inquire. Lace, fish, love (or what they call "love"), pajanche (*i.e.*, money), pojenta (*i.e.*, eating and drinking), and occasional kinemato-graphs, are the only subjects which the Buranello intellect ever seriously tackles. The crowd dispersed with grave salutations, returning to its beverages and games of cards and *dama*.

About twenty minutes later, the sindaco, Sior Bon, whose gentility I here wish to acknowledge, brought me (very quietly and submysteriously) a tottering piscatorial survivor from unbelievable antiquity, rheumy-nosed, blear-eyed, knobby-as-to-the-articulations, whom he described as a touch of poor old male with a little information. I instantly called for a half-litre of black brusk for him, and waited for the usual silly lies invariably offered out of courtesy to strangers.

"Sior," says he, "in the first beginning that island there which his Sioria has seen was the cemetery for all the islands of this lagoon here, north of Murano. But when we made our cemetery at Mazorbo near here, then that old one was abandoned and became the abode of owls and phantasms. And when we had liberated Italy, which God willed, then after, the Government told us to go and clear away the cadavers of those drunkards, buffoons, and other obscene Germans from the battlefields on the mainlands, and to jet them somewhere out of sight, so that the honest peasants of the vineyards of *terra firma* might be no longer annoyed by them and their putrid stenches. And there was what I wish to call a regiment of us working for a year or more to do it thoroughly, with *burchi* and *peate* and *topi* and all kinds of *barche* out of the Arsenal of Venice, which the Government lent to us. And we took the accursed Tedeschi, thousands of them and all foetid, and we flung them on to our abandoned cemetery, spitting on them naturally, Host! but not wishing to do them ultimate discourtesy by refusing them a resting-place on sanctified earth. Sior, I pray!"

And all that night I dreamed of the long black serpents sinuously streaming out of the eye-holes of Austrian skulls. Ouph! I can see them now.

# ON CASCADING INTO THE CANAL

## (JULY 1913)

I EMPHATICALLY affirm that this is not a habit of mine. I have only done it once, so far; and I have not the slightest intention of doing it again of my own free will.

All gondoglieri, and most mothers, butt their babies into the canal long before the age of reason, to teach them to swim. For, notwithstanding the municipal warning which afflicts every street-corner, "*Divieto di nuoto*" *i.e.*, "Swimming is Prohibited," people who cannot swim don't have much of a time in Venice—if one can believe the local *Gazzettino*, which every week reports the "*disgrazia*" or misfortune of some "povero diavolo che di soddisfare ad un naturale bisogno" (that is to say, of some poor devil who to satisfy a natural want) poises himself on a canal edge and topples in, always to a nasty wetting, and sometimes (when drunk and alone at midnight) to a damp death. Swimming, consequently, is almost universally practised. Any fine summer evening, as you creep up the Grand Canal in your gondogla, little pink shrimps of urchins will slip off steps, and swim festively a little way with you. In the large canals quite

big boys, *juvenes vegeto corpore viridi et robusto*, will dive terrifically off bridges, for the admiration of female cous-
ins and the sisters of chums. And, if you penetrate into
smaller waterways, you certainly will encounter respectable (but unabashed) mothers of large families in their
nightgowns, placidly brooding for coolness' sake up to
their necks in water among the crabs on their bottom
doorsteps. But, to speak precisely, I only saw five persons
(beside myself) cascade accidentally into the canal during
my first two years here; and I am on the water at least five
days a week all the time.

The first was a happy (but inebriated) old hooker of
*gondogle*, who rolled in one night by the station, and pas-
sionately invoked "Oysters!"—"Ostreghe!" the pious
Venetian euphemism for The Host, *i.e.*, "Ostia!"—absolutely declining to come out till someone would guaran-
tee him another little beaker (bicchierino). And the mob
good-humouredly derided him, and left him wallowing:
as also did I.

The second was a young gondogliere of mine called
Rinaldo Galli. It was my first winter in Venice, and before I myself began (of necessity) to follow the art and
mystery of the oar. The Universal Infirmary, at that time,
had a directress of fiercely prominent social attainments,
which led her to enliven the dull season by competing
with our Sailors' Institute in the matter of the amusement of mariners, gaining the local name of "Casino Inglese" for the pious foundation over which she otherwise
acceptably presided. In this connection, I carried her
and a nurse and a dirty white poodle (creeping with mi-
crobes) in my *barcheta*, on the 23rd of December, round

all the English ships then lying in the harbour of Marit-
tima, delivering personal invitations to the officers to
attend a friendly sing-song with pantomimes and slight
refreshments at the Infirmary on the ensuing Boxing
Night. The weather was windy, the wide canal of Zuecca
distinctly billowy: but we fought our way round some
twenty ships without mishap, and we parted at the last,
a coal-tramp, which lay by the coal-heaps at the mouth
of Rio San Basegio, I to return to my club, the matron
and nurse to go on foot through the city to take tea in
Dorsoduro. So far, I have nothing to complain of. But
the next morning, Christmas Eve, I presented myself as
usual at the Infirmary for orders. (Having a commodious
*barcheta*, a lust for outdoor exercise, a will to make myself
useful for no reward, and a most fastidious contempt for
appearances, I was the Infirmary's gushed-upon handy-
man in those days.) And my horror can perhaps be im-
agined when the directress confronted me with agonised
demands for her infernal poodle. I had thought that she
had taken it with her the day before to Ca' Pacello. She,
on her part, had had the conscience to think that I had
made the whole voyage over again, against both wind
and tide, simply to transport the filthy creature home to
the English Casino—I beg pardon, I mean the Universal
Infirmary—before taking my well-earned ease in my club.
Anyhow, the beast was lost, the directress heartbroken
without her foot-warmer, and mine was the delicious job
of retrieving him. And the weather was simply abominable. The Zuecca Canal swelled and rolled and gave itself
airs quite nastily; and we had to recross it, and to struggle
right down to the other end of it. My *barcheta* was by no

means a thirsty boat: but I'm bound to say she shipped more than one sea that day. I intended to begin inquiries with the coal-tramp, and to work back from her: so I landed among the coal-heaps on the quay by Rio San Basegio, leaving my gondogliere Rinaldo on the *puppa* of the *barcheta*, while I ascended the tramp's black side to ask whether they had seen a poodle. They had, by George! "Have you come for your dog, sir? Because we sail in five minutes and have just put him ashore." Thus the steward. I thanked him in the usual manner for entertaining the truant all night, and climbed back to earth to search among the coal-heaps. Of course the beast came frolicking up instantly, very pleased to see me (all poodles being the most self-incriminating fools); and equally, of course, he was as black as the Bride in the Canticle, *nigra sum sed formosa*, though by no means so comely. I swore, and took him in my arms to get back to the *barcheta*; and, lo, there was that blighter of a Rinaldo, as black as ink also, wringing himself out on the poop, having cascaded improvisedly into the coaly canal. "And why?" I demanded. "I don't know nothing about nothing—mi no co gnente de gnente" was his plenary confession of ignorance, which left me to opine that he had bathed out of sheer absence of mind. He was that species of person, and (being a Venetian) eminently complacent about himself. There was nothing for me to do but to sweat him heavily at his oar till we had returned the bacterio poodle to the Infirmary, where I begged a tot of brandy for him, and sent him home to dry.

The third occurred at a funeral in February. The second engineer of s.s. *Elswick Manor* died of pneumonia in the Infirmary, and we buried his remains at San Michele, on the other side of Venice. I saw the coffin placed on the funereal gondogla, covered with the banner of England, and then (I being a poor benighted papist, and afraid that they would shoo me off if I attempted to assist at an Erastian function) went ahead of the procession in my *barcheta*, and a string of *gondogle* containing the chaplain and sundry mourning mates and captains followed after. We trailed across the wide Zuecca Canal and the Basin of Saint Mark, entering the swift current of Rio del Palazzo. But, after passing under the Bridge of Sighs, and just as we were about to turn to the right, my boy (Marcoleone this time) yelled from the poop behind me, "Sior, sior, do the pleasure of regarding the gondogliere who has cascaded into the canal!" I drew in my prow-oar, and switched me round to see. Sure enough, disaster had overtaken the steersman of the first gondogla of captains. He had toppled off his poop, in such a moment of madness as may come to the best of us when we are a little cheerful, and was swimming vociferously to the steps by Pauly's small bridge, while his comrade of the prow-oar was hopping nimbly along the gunwale to correct the meanderings of the gondogla. Instantly, papist or not, I had my *barcheta* laid alongside the now half-manned ship, into which I promptly skipped, and rowed its prow-oar in the procession to the cemetery, leaving Marcoleone to follow me at leisure, to the joy of the English captains.

The fourth happened in May. I was spending a rainy night walking to and fro on the Zattere, pretending that I liked being homeless and penniless, and telling the Signiors of the Night (who inquired) that I was studying the effects of night-lights and the whiteness of dawn. All was as black as pitch. A quarter of a mile away, on the other side of the canal, were the daffodil-coloured dots of the lamps outlining the long island of Zuecca, shining through an old silver-coloured mesh of falling rain. The quay of the Zattere, where I was, is not ins-esthetically illuminated. Electric arc-lamps do not defile it. The municipality of Venice is Clerico-Socialist, but decent taste is not invariably absent from its perform-ances. It gives us just enough unremarkable gas-lamps to show where land ends and water begins; and no sober, well-meaning wanderer ever need cascade inadvertently into canals. I walked up and down and up and down the mile-long quay, observing the last ferries starting to cross to Zuecca after 1 a.m., and the various tipsy persons who intoned dismal ditties containing precise details of the fate of "ragazzine die fanno l'amore." And presently, af-ter about an hour of silence, a pallid, long youth leaped out of a shadow by the bridge over Rio di San Trovaso, averring that he had that moment heard the groan and the splash of a man in the water. I looked over the para-pet with some interest. "*Non solum me numen et implaoabile fatum Persequitur.*" I wasn't the only person in the world who was up a tree, then. But it was too dark to see even a sign of a ripple. "Here," says I, "you just come along and tell your tale to a Signior of the Night." [The "Nocturnal Guard" is a private police maintained by a commercial firm in the city. You pay a small fee to the firm, and be-come frightfully bucked at having your letter-box filled and your doors and windows plastered with licked tick-ets, testifying how many times each night your fastenings have been tried by your protectors. Also, I understand, the Nocturnal Guards take note of suicides, &c., summoning medical guards and civil guards when necessary for the arrest of satyrs, drunkards, buffoons, Germans, and other obscenities.] We found a *Guardia Notturna*, and duly advised him. I cannot conceive anything more disinterested than his demeanour. "Only some inebriated *barcajuolo* washing his feet," was his opinion, though I'm bound to say he came quite promptly to investigate the scene. As for the pallid, long youth, he was a prey to such frightful excitement that his mind gave signs of becoming unhinged. Also he was half-starved. I myself, being in a verisimilar condition that night, was painfully aware of the mental horror which grows upon a fecund male who sees God solemnly going round in awful pomp and solemnly slamming every door in his face excepting the magenta one which leads to suicide. Therefore I experienced an active sympathy with the poor boy's agitation, and began to undo my buttons and bootlaces, in case it should be necessary for me to salve a body out of that canal. But first, having two halfpenny rolls ("*cioppi*") and two penny packets of indigenous cigarettes, I shared them with the pallid, long youth, by way of soothing him. Do you, oh most affable reader, know what it feels like when your bowels of compassion yearn? He was so ravenously hungry that he wolfed down my two dry, uninteresting lumps of bread before I had time to scratch up enough selfishness to refrain me from pressing them upon him. Then we stood on the bridge a minute or two, looking at the dark water. Up the Rio di San Trovaso, the old *squero* silhouetted itself in dark black on pale black.

And suddenly, from nowhere in particular, but from somewhere quite near, came an unmistakable indrawn breath with the out-shot breath which follows it and is a groan. It was quite ghastly. I coursed wildly off the bridge and along the *fondamenta* on the right side of the little Rio, undoing my remaining buttons, and preparing such pluck as I possessed for doing an uninviting though distinct deed. But the voice of the frightened boy on the bridge called me back. A staggering portent was sloppily passing him, trailing seaweed and oozing moisture, and humped together like some monstrous glistening antediluvian snail, whom the Nocturnal Guard instantly required to decline his generalities. Most straightforward these were. Arcangelo Zabajon, called Bon, aged 27, a "casalingo," *i.e.*, a lingerer-at-home (which seems to be a recognised profession in Venice), had sat on the steps of the doctor's Watergate at the west end of the bridge for a purpose, and, accidentally, had cascaded into the canal, whence he immediately retracted himself: but, hearing voices near, and not having the courage to face criticism (which seems to be recognised as a perfectly legitimate excuse for many faults in Venice), he had hidden in the shadow till the cold and the wet struck him as being intolerable. Whereupon he emerged, intending to go to his home in the Earthed River of the Catechumens—*Rio Terrà dei Catecumeni,*—and so, "Siori, buona notte." And that was all about that.

The fifth happened in June. It was full summer; and the victim was an English artist, whom I was obliged to serve as gondogliere. We set out to make a day of it on the lagoon, lunching at the island of Saint George among the seaweeds, and then passing under the railway bridge, right round by the Fondamenta Nuova to the Arsenal. And, near this last, but I will not indicate precisely where (nor would it be much good if I did, seeing that the spot is now entirely obliterated by the new naval dry dock), we found a deep and unobserved place, which simply sang to us to come and bathe. I went in first, to demonstrate how headers must be taken off a dancing *barcheta*, and how one has to heave oneself in-board again. Next, my employer enacted an atrocious belly-flopper, and wallowed in the sportful brine. It was all quite all right. After we were dressed, the plan being to return slowly to Palazzo del Angelo *viâ* Castello and the Biva degli Schiavoni, I took my poop-oar and began again to row. Wind, here, was against me, current was fiercely against me, progress was very slow. At the now-covered corner of the Arsenal it was awful. I, sweating, swore beneath my breath. "Get over to that *palo* there, and tie up and rest a bit," says my merciful master to his beast. I thankfully obeyed. He rose, with the cord in his hand, ready to take a turn round the indicated post when I reached it. Slowly I forged across the flood. The *palo* appeared near. The *barcheta* touched it, and I glided her along it. My *paron* seized it, embraced it, began to encircle it with the cord. *Pudet referre quca sequuntur*, but the appalling catastrophe suddenly occurred thus. My master (a robust piece of man, with the port and aspect of the Erastian curate who plays cricket with hooligans on Sundays and boxes them every night of the week), hung on to the post with his arms embracing it, his legs in the vanishing boat, and the most touching expression of innocence mingled with devotion which

I ever have seen on any human countenance excepting the infant Samuel's. His knees crooked. Away whirled the *barcheta*, twisted by wind and tide, both shrieking with laughter. And, with puffy cheeks, shut eyes, and a meek splosh, my employer cascaded into the canal. Of course I got the naughty craft alongside of the site of his disappearance, and, when his head popped up, I told him to hang on to the gunwale till I could draw him into water sufficiently shallow for him (weighted with his wet clothes) to crawl in. Another *barcheta*, rowed by friars minor from San Francesco del Deserto, went by with unctuous and most uufranciscan disgust. Blessed Brother Francis would have joined in our merriment; they did not even proffer Extreme Unction. Ensued a wildly fantastic toilette. I hung my *paron's* wet garments on the peak of the *porcola* to drain, while I lent him my spare sweater (fearfully and wonderfully *décolleté* it was on him), and my spare sandals (Pompeian pattern and vermilion), and my white linen hat, in place of which last I wound a white-silk neck-square round my head, making myself look like an erudite but otherwise honest Jesuit posing as one of Brangwyn's brigands—so my master declared. You are not to think, however, that he (amiable, placid man) pervaded the *rii* of Venice vested solely in the airy fashion just described. Beside my sweater and sandals and hat, he embellished his manly torso with a dry dustcoat of his own, while an old burberry weather-proof of mine piously veiled his chubby knees. And, in this garb, he demanded his tea—a hilarious repast consisting of egg-and-cucumber sandwiches, with red wine and cigarettes—after which we turned and went back with the tide, passing through small canals, which extend inward from the Rio dei Mendicanti. It was a voyage richly punctuated with chuckles on the part of both of us. I know that we exposed a spectacle as startling as a carnival, but the Venetians understand that we English (though rolling in gold, and therefore admirable) are stark staring mad; and the sight of one in two coats, a low-necked sweater, vermilion sandals, and a white linen hat, and of another coifed like a pirate and doing gondogliere, simply struck them still and speechless. No one even spat over a bridge on us. No one even tittered when we reached the palace, and my *paron* had to skip pink-leggedly over a barge of ice-blocks moored to his own Watergate. But all ended well, and I did not lose my situation.

I suppose we English do not habitually blame where blame is not actually due. My master did not. And I'm sure I don't. I was thrown out of my own *barcheta* by my own gondogliere last November, and I did not fire the boy for it.

It was bleak and misty autumn, late in a cheerless afternoon. I had been writing at the Club "Bucintoro," and I decided to freshen myself up with a turn on the water before going home to tea. My gondogliere then was a certain Einilio Sacripan, naturally called "Emily," a very fine fellow indeed, magnificently breasted and throated, and quite picturesque poised on pointed feet on my lofty poop. He was, however, an unpunctual, untrustworthy little devil, and had been in disgrace with me so often that I seriously told him to beware of erring again before the month's end, on penalty of having either to take such a thrashing *modo Inglese* as would prevent him from sitting comfortably for a fortnight, or else to receive licence to quit my service. He was dismal in consequence, not liking the idea of being whipped by what he called a "forester," and going in the bluest of funks of the tipsy father who lived on his earnings, and certainly would beat him senseless if he lost his situation. So he was on his best behaviour when we set forth that dull cold afternoon on the top of a high tide and a flowing sea, from the Club, up Canal Grande past La Salute, turning off at the Duchess of Madrid's red and yellow posted palace with the gilded Florentine lilies, to go up Rio di San Vio. [By the bye, why mix gilding with yellow paint in an heraldic achievement, when *Or* is signified? And why Florentine lilies instead of Bourbon? For surely Don Carlos was a Bourbon.] And then, just after you pass the Erastian temple, the Rio di San Vio narrows, and is crossed by a bridge, before it widens again into a very decent canal with quays for pedestrians on both sides of it. We had swirled through the narrow part and under the bridge, when the calamity occurred. I was rowing at the prow, and Emily was steering at the poop, the pace being my usual swift and hectic one. A big unwieldy barca of firewood came suddenly towards us, rowed by two of my former gondoglieri, Piero Veneraud and Ermenegildo Vianel, who had gotten a better winter job than mine in the firewood business of the latter's father. To avoid collision, Emily precipitately twitched my *barcheta* to one side without much judgment. I incontinently lost my balance; and, disliking the notion of crashing ignominiously in-board to sprawl among oars and *forcole*, I made no ado whatever, but just gripped my short pipe more tightly between my teeth, and took a neat header into the canal, passing right under the approaching wood barge. As I shot through the air I saw all the hands of all the people on the two *fondamente* being flung to heaven, and I heard all their voices bawling, "Ara, Ara! O Maria vergine! For pleasure here is an English going to drown himself fastidiously!" So, as soon as I got under water, I told myself that the said English had better give these people something truly rare and wholesome to cough about. Wherefore I swam, submerged, about thirty yards up the Rio, passionlessly emerging (to a fanfare of yells) in a totally unexpected place, with a perfectly stony face, and the short pipe still stiff and rigid in an immovable mouth. The crowd increased with augmented hullabalooing. I merely floated expressionlessly as a frog. That wretched Emily precipitated the *barcheta* toward me in a most horrible state of alarm about his situation. Instant and shameful dismissal on the spot was the only mercy which he expected. All kinds of other *barcajuoli* hurried up, specially the enchanting Piero Venerand, *queo de le tre rose mi su 'l capeo*, and between them I became splendidly retrieved from the flood and set on foot in my own boat, still immutably solemn, and weeping streams from every edge of my habiliments. I slowly wiped my monocle on the cushions and stuck it in its place. My every movement was watched intensely. Emilio's agitated devotion was a choice thing to remember. I deliberately surveyed my surroundings with the weird, somewhat annoyed, unseeing, somnambulistic glare of a priest scurrying past Christ's poor in the absence of a newspaper reporter. And then, as though performing some ritual function, I knocked the wet tobacco out of my pipe over the gunwale. Hundreds of arms seemed to shoot out to assist me. I extracted a sodden India rubber pouch from my wet pocket; and "Somebody with dry hands will, for gentility's sake, favour me by proving whether the tobacco herein is still lightable," I grimly intoned. Thousands of somebodies seemed to do so. It was. "For pleasure replenish me this pipe," I gravely continued. "Old That!" shrieked a shawled hag on the *fondamenta* to her mate, "those English there will smoke their pipes even when they quit their deathbeds for the embrace of Mariavergine!" And it seemed as though millions of voices roared prophecies in stentorian chorus to the effect that I was certainly going the very best way to catch a stroke of air, if not a pulmonitis. "Mah!" I snorted to them, with the impregnable, contemptuous indifference of a basalt god. And, "Somebody with dry hands will favour me with a lighted match," I chanted again in a gaunt and colourless monotone. There was a sudden sort of pyrotechnic display, as everybody's *fiammiferi* flamed. I selected the longest and flamingest. I lighted my pipe. I resumed my oar. And, "Go on, dear thou," I said holily to Emily. "But that, what English!" exclaimed the crowd as we swirled away up the Rio, and out into the canal of Zuecca, and round by the Custom House to the club again, rowing like demons to keep my blood from freezing. And then I took a douche and changed into dry flannels, while Emilio comforted me with coffee and curaçao. He would have offered the tray on his knees if I had permitted it.

# VENETIAN COURTESY

## (SEPTEMBER 1913)

IN early October I pottered about the north lagoon in my *barcheta*. The weather was so deliciously like full summer that I made no change in my customs, but continued to live in the open while writing Mr X's third book for him. I ought to explain that my own irrefrainable energy, and a series of circumstances, and a coming-together of a parcel of unscrupulous scoundreloids, had made me a "Literary Ghost." I wrote (or rewrote) other people's bad books; and eminent publishers innocently published my work under the incapable authors' names. One must do something—at least, I must,—and though, as a Ghost, one earns less than a pound a week and the most hideous reputation, still, one pegs on, till the blissful day when one has snaffled an opportunity of publishing beautiful absolute works of one's very own.

I came to Venice in August for a six weeks' holiday; and lived and worked and slept in my *barcheta* almost always. It seemed that, by staying on, I could most virtuously and most righteously cheat autumn and winter. Such was the effect of this kind of Venetian life on me,

that I felt no more than twenty-five years old, in everything excepting valueless experience and valuable disillu-
sion. The bounding joy of vigorous health, the physical
capacity for cheerful (nay, gay) endurance, the careless,
untroubled mental activity, the perfectly gorgeous ap-
petite, the prompt, delicate, dreamless nights of sleep,
which betoken healthy youth,—all this (with indescribable happiness) I had triumphantly snatched from solitude
with the sun and the sea. I went swimming half a dozen
times a day, beginning at white dawn, and ending after
sunsets which set the whole lagoon ablaze with amethyst
and topaz. Between friends, I will confess that I am not
guiltless of often getting up in the night and popping
silently overboard to swim for an hour in the clear of
a great gold moon—plenilunio—or among the waving
reflections of the stars. (O my goodness me, how heavenly a spot that is!) When I wanted change of scene and
anchorage, I rowed with my two gondoglieri; and there is
nothing known to physiculturists (for giving you "poise"
and the organs and figure of a slim young Diadymenos)
like rowing standing in the Mode Venetian. It is jolly hard
work; but no other exercise bucks you up as does spring-
ing forward from your toe-tips and stretching forward
to the full in pushing the oar, or produces such exquisite
lassitude at night when your work is done. And I wrote
quite easily for a good seven hours each day. Could anything be more felicitous?

And, one day, I replenished my stock of provisions at
Burano; and at sunset we rowed away to find a station for
the night. Imagine a twilight world of cloudless sky and
smoothest sea, all made of warm, liquid, limpid helio-

trope and violet and lavender, with bands of burnished copper set with emeralds, melting, on the other hand, into the fathomless blue of the eyes of the prides of peacocks, where the moon rose, rosy as mother-of-pearl. Into such glory we three advanced the black *barcheta*, solemnly, silently, when the last echo of Avemmaria died.

Slowly we came out north of Burano into the open lagoon; and rowed eastward to meet the night, as far as the point marked by five *pali*, where the wide canal curves to the south. Slowly we went. There was something so holy—so majestically holy—in that evening silence, that I would not have it broken even by the quiet plash of oars. I was lord of time and place. No engagement cried to be kept. I could go when and where I pleased, fast or slow, far or near. And I chose the near and the slow. I did more. So unspeakably gorgeous was the peace on the lagoon just then, that it inspired me with a lust for doing nothing at all but sitting and absorbing impressions motionlessly. That way come thoughts, new, generally noble.

The wide canal, in which we drifted, is a highway. I have never seen it unspeckled by the *sandoli* of Buranelli fishers. Steam-boats, and tank-barges of fresh water for Burano, and the ordinary barks of carriage, disturb it, not always, but often. My wish was to find a smaller canal, away—away. We were (as I said) at the southern side, at the southward curve marked by five *pali*. Opposite, on the other bank, begins the long line of *pali* which shows the deep-water way right down to the Ricevitoria of Treporti; and there, at the beginning of the line, I spied the mouth of a canal which seemed likely to suit me. We rowed across to it, and entered. It tended north-eastward for two or three hundred metres, and then bended like an elbow north-westward. It looked quite a decent canal, perhaps forty metres in width, between sweet mud-banks clothed with sea-lavender about two-foot lengths above high-water mark in places. We pushed inshore, near to the inner bank at the elbow, stuck a couple of oars into the mud fore and aft, and moored there.

Baicolo and Caicio got out the draught-board and cigarettes, and played below their breath on the *puppa*; while I sat still, bathing my soul in peace, till the night was dark and Selene high in the limpid sapphire-blue. Then they lighted the *fanali*, and put up the impermeable awning with wings and curtains to cover the whole *barcheta*; and made a Parmentier soup to eat with our wine and *polenta*. And, when kapok-cushions had been arranged on the floor, and summer sleeping-bags laid over them, we took our last dash overboard, said our prayers, and went to bed. Baicola at *prova* with his feet toward mine amidships, and Caioio under the *puppa* with his feet well clear of my pillowed head. So, we slept.

Soon after sunrise I awakened: it was a sunrise of opal and fire: the boys were deep in slumber. I took down the awning, and unmoored quietly, and mounted the *puppa* to row about in the dewy freshness in search of a fit place for my morning plunge. I am very particular about this. Deep water I must have—as deep as possible—I being what the Venetians call "appassionato per l'acqua." Beside that, I have a vehement dyspathy against getting entangled in weed or in mud, to make my toe-nails dirtier than my fingernails. And, being congenitally myopic, I see more clearly in deep water than in shallow, almost as clearly, in fact, as with a concave monocle on land. So I left the *barcheta* to drift with the current, while I took soundings with the long oar of the *puppa*, in several parts of the canal, near both banks as well as in the middle. Nowhere could I touch bottom; and this signified that my bathing-place was more than four metres in depth. Needless to say that I gave a joyful morning yell, which dragged from sleep the luxury-loving Baicolo to make coffee, and the faithful dog Caicio to take my oar and keep the *barcheta* near me; and then I plunged overboard to revel in the limpid green water. Lord, how lovely is Thy smooth salt sea flowing on flesh!

When I heaved myself in-board again, the ship was cleared and tidied for the day, and the coffee ready. I spread a towel on cushions and sprawled to dry in the sun while I sipped. The boys dived and swam, returning to take their refreshment while I rolled the day's first cigarette.

After we had gotten into our shorts and zephyrs, the awning was put up against the increasing sun-blaze; and I opened my paper-case, beginning to think about my morning's writing. Baicolo and Caicio did little odd jobs of polishing brass and steel work and scraping the oars, to whiten them, with broken shreds of glass. But first it occurred to me to look at my chart of the lagoon to find the name of the exquisite canal where I lay—the canal which had all desirable qualities of depth and width and about a chilometre of length, emerging northward by a delta in the Canale Dossa Piccola, which goes to my island full of skeletons. Also, it had wide, wide views in every direction, was very private and concealed (by its curves) from highways, and at the same time it was not half an hour's row from Burano. In brief, an ideal camping-place—lonely, lovely, free, and within easy reach of fresh bread and water and salads. And on my chart there was no trace of it, excepting a dwarfed and nameless mouth of it beginning just before the first palo of the main canal, running north-eastward about a hundred metres, and then losing itself miserably in the great Marsh of the Sentrega. I was much annoyed.

I was very much annoyed, because only the week before I had found a high, large grassy island (an abode of rats) north of the canal highway from Venice to the mainland at San Giuliano, and close to that hamlet, but altogether unmarked on my official chart. I was, in fact, frightfully annoyed, because there could be no possible shadow of a doubt about my latest find being long and wide and deep, and much more important than innumerable little canals not more than ten metres wide and a metre (or less) in depth, which the same chart sedulously indicated. I took a second survey, verified my previous impressions, and became aware that there was no writing other people's books possible for me that day.

"To Venice, suddenly, where I shall attend to my affairs, while you may have liberty to 'far festa' and to salute your genitors and to view the kinematographs," said I to my gondoglieri.

We reached the city in time for lunch. The boys emptied the *barcheta* and made all secure before they scampered away. I changed into clean flannels, and went to Ascension to cough at Ongania Amadeo (seller of my charts), asking whether he was sure that he had not sold me obsolete ones. He consulted the official list of charts of the Estuario Veneto issued by the Hydrographic Institute, and showed me that mine, being dated 1905, were then the very latest. I think he was a little upset by my polite insinuation; but when I told him about the unmarked island by San Giuliano, and of the canal across the Palude della Sentrega, he became interested. And (let me tell you) an interested Venetian can be extremely interesting, almost as interesting as a sailor. In that short conversation I learned unheard of and undreamed of mysteries about the vagaries of the lagoon, its shifting mud-banks, its daily changing channels.

"But this island and this canal which His Signoria has found seem to be permanent and important, and I beg that he will so far disturb himself as to pass by the Hydrographic Department of the Arsenal and to speak of these high matters with my friend Commandant Angelo Francon, who has them in charge," said Amadeo Ongania.

So I strolled up to the Arsenal, and found a large and full commandant, with fine clear eyes, a cigarette, and the calmest and strongest of manners—just the sort of commandant to become one of the heroes of the Libyan campaign, as he did subsequently. Out of sheer selfish laziness I asked whether he understood English. He replied in that tongue, speaking quite fluently and beautifully, but so deliberately and so absolutely without any kind of emphasis that all his syllables seemed to be hyphened together with a comma after each. "Yes-," he said, "I-, can-, un-, der-, stand-, Eng-, lish-, if-, you-, will-, have-, the-, ve-, ry-, great-, kind-, ness-, to-, speak-, as-, slow-, ly-, as-, pos-, si-, ble-, and-, I-, can-, speak-, it-, al-, so-, if-, you-, will-, per-, mit-, me-, to-, speak-, like-, this."

We got on splendidly at once. He was simpaticissimo. I showed my passport: said that I was an English writer who preferred to live and write on the lagoon for the sake of health and solitude, and that I had accidentally made a pair of small discoveries which (thought Ongania) might be useful to the official hydrographers. And I displayed my chart, indicating in pencil the situations of the unmarked island and canal.

The Commandant sent for his Department's copy of the chart. To our amusement it turned out to be an even earlier edition than mine—the edition of 1903, I think. We exchanged the usual polite commiserations on the abominable way in which all departments of all governments always neglect each other, and then he carefully traced my amateur pencil-marks from my chart, for professional transference to his, and assured me that the Hydrographic Ship should be sent to verify and measure and sound and survey, so that the next issue of the chart might be brought thoroughly up to date.

"But be pleased to tell me, sir," he said, in his slow, sure English, "how did you form so clear an opinion of the depth and width and length of this canal?"

At this I laughed, and confessed my diving propensities, and my performances with the long oar of my *puppa*. Then we shared compliments—and parted. I must say that the manners of all Italian officials known to me are quite delightful. They are keen and business-like; but they are charmingly courteous and human withal. They do not shunt or snub you, but take a really pleasing personal interest in you. I remember a Quaestor (before whom I once had to testify concerning a doubtful young person, thrown in my way by the Erastian Thiasarkh of Venice) who came down precipitately from his bench, when he heard that literature was my profession, to beg for the pleasure of shaking my hand, on the ground that his own much respected father (Poareto! R.I.P.) had also been a man of letters.

It rained that night. The glass in Saint Mark's Square went down; and the observatory of the Patriarchal Semi-nary predicted a few days' inclemency. So I gave my gon-doglieri a "festive repose," and shut myself up at home, to go on with my disgusting job of planting and watering (like Paul and Apollos) for somebody else to reap.

Two mornings later I got a note from Commandant Francon, asking me to do him the gentility of receiving him that evening at 18 o'clock. I replied that I should be most happy; and prayed him to stay and dine at 19.30. He answered with a second note, begging for reception at 18, and regretting inability to dine. I moaned, but assented.

He arrived punctually. His uniform was most care-ful and aesthetic, his salutation magnificent. His man-ner was as calm and weighty and trustworthy as at our first meeting, but it had also a certain authority, a certain formality.

He said that his happy mission was to convey to me the thanks of the Vice-Admiral commanding the Port for the information which I had so obligingly brought to the Hydrographic Department of the Arsenal. I simpered.

Then he moved to the chair which I was offering him, sat down affably, and drew off his lovely white gloves, and every single scrap of formality with them. I seated myself near him, and protruded cigarettes.

"I must ask you to pardon me, dear sir," he said, still gravely, "for not accepting your genteel invitation to dinner. And I pray you to believe what I am about to tell you. May I hope that you will favour me with this gentility?"

I said that, like Saint Anselm of England, it was my habit to believe, simply in order that I might understand. "*Credo ut intelligam.*" It was the best way known to me of sparing myself unnecessary intellectual obfuscation.

"Then, dear sir," he continued," you will know that it is not suitable to mingle duty with pleasure. My mission was official, if you permit me to say so."

I permitted.

"But, apart from that, though I do not look like a sick man, I am but just recovered from a putrid malady; and I assure you that it is a fact that my doctors force me to a diet which precludes me from ever eating with other people, and deprives me altogether of my dinner."

I condoled.

Here the last trace of his gravity also became wiped out. His dismissal, first of his official authority, and now of his by no means unbecoming seriousness, had precisely the effect of taking off his tunic and collar with the notion of spending an easy evening with me in his shirt-sleeves. I also hastened to divest my manner of any frills which might by chance be still embellishing it.

"And now, dear thou," he surprisingly went on, "I have something else to say which is not official and not polite. It is not Commandant Francon who speaks to thee now. It is not even that poor convalescent imploring pardon for refusing to eat thy tasty dinner. But I am going to say something to thee, not as an Italian to an English who is so genteel as to listen to him, not as between foreigners, but as between two men of the world who are very great friends. Thou understandest? Thou dost permit it? Dear thou, thy friend, not Commandant Francon, but thy friend here, says then to thee, not officially, but privately, and in the very purest friendship, 'Dear friend, please do not measure any more of our canals, because it would give me such a pain if thou wert to get thyself into trouble."

"But" (with a bounce) "have I been putting myself in contravention? Of course you know that I have no intention of an evil kind. Besides, dear friend, we English are the best friends of you Italians, though you have chosen to ally yourselves with dyspathetic Germans. Certainly, I myself am. And, when I make discoveries—and an observant man of my species cannot help making discoveries,—naturally I make a present of them to you. That is your right." Thus I, excited, but tickled.

"Dearest of loyal friends, I know it all," continued the Commandant. "I am not saying any ugly word like 'contravention.' But all the lagoon is under military jurisdiction. Thou knowest it? And thou knowest why? The Trentino? Vereto Giulia? Ours, by Bacchus! Isn't it true? Thy sympathy is with us? Ah, thou art truly an English! Well, dear friend, in out-of-the-way parts of the lagoon, which thy singular eminent genius leads thee to admire and to frequent, thou mightst be interrupted in measuring canals, and molested, and misunderstood, by countrified but zealous guards. And conceive how grieved thy friend would be on hearing that thou hadst been forced so to incommode thyself as to have to come specially to Venice to furnish stupid officials with explanations. It is not for me to say how grieved the Vice-Admiral would be. It is enough that I, thy friend, would be grieved extremely, chagrined, desolated, to think that thou shouldst find thyself in so displeasing and so pietose a situation. Dear friend, then, send me away with a soul secure against such grief. Tell me that thou wilt not annoy thyself by being caught measuring our canals."

I burst into inextinguishable laughter as we both stood up. "Oh, I think you are the most charming and the most exquisite people in the world. I'm a bit of a Machiavelli myself, and I am so glad that I am friendly with you," I exclaimed. "Pray, valiant Commandant, convey my respectful thanks to the Vice-Admiral for his altogether undeserved recognition of me. And pray, dear friend, accept also my most sincere thanks for the delicate courtesy of your warning. I promise not to measure any more of your canals, excepting to assure myself that I shall not imbed my head in mud when diving. Will that satisfy you?"

"Admirably!" declared Commandant Francon.

# THE TATTOOED WEDDING RING

(OCTOBER 1897)

OF the suggesting that weddings rings of men as well as women tattooed should be, maniac female, the blood, desire.

She, by, before the public eye in the *Pall Mall Gazette*, a wild hideous fantasy of her, like the Athenian always something new seeking, brain, putting; me, who even her have seen, much less to her a wrong have done, the well-known high born loving friend of my manhood, not than my youth less, to lose has made.

I the sad story tell will.

Rudolph my friend, in pocket as the Job of you poor was, but of pure gold of him the brain always has been, and of medicine the science, in this of yours rich country, he to practise came. But he for a diploma the money no-how raise could. Then Rudolph, with that of gold brain, to Nancy, hypnotism to learn, he would go, said; because a diploma, in this of yours rich country, hypnotism to practise, necessary not is; and by it one way or another, of money lots, made can be. But when he, how the trick, at this thumb-nail people to stare, by making, to do, had learned; from Nancy returned Rudolph, and a man him chambers to lend persuaded; where he patients received, and hypnotically them treated. The wonders that he did, you your eyes open would make; for he a patient in the Park would meet; and:

"Sleep; to me a bob my railway-fare to pay, lend," would say, and the patient meekly a silver shilling to Rudolph hand would. And to another patient, he a telegram, "pay my gas-bill," saying, would send; whereupon the patient two golden sovereigns out would fork.

*Ach Himmel*, that I a such friend have lost.

And one day, Rudolph, his round face with good sausage shining and with joy beaming, to me came; and that he, of a fine fat fräulein of your Yorkshire County, the heart had won, said; and that as she rich was, when he her married had, we both her money upon could live, added. So I upon his neck fell, and with all my heart kissed, and hocks how many we drank I to tell am unable.

In course of time, to her his best beloved, he with pride rotund and gay, me did introduce; that I of his youth the companion and of his manhood the heart-brother was, saying. And I, myself agreeable and entertaining to Rudolph's bride-to-be to make, myself exerted, and all of London City the glories to her described.

She, me of her Rudolph the heart-friend, like gospel believed; and when the, whose arterial blood for black puddings I require maniac female, a march upon the Editor of the *Pall Mall Gazette* stole; and, that henceforth tattooed wedding rings the thing to be were, proclaimed; she, that is the sweetest idea was, declared, and the loyal love-blinded Rudolph so too declared; and nothing, but that at their wedding they both a finger tattooed should

have, would do. Her uncle, the clergyman who them to
marry had promised, a Ritualist was, and he too, of the
most touching and beautiful the idea to be, pronounced.
It, him, of one of the rites sacramental of the ancient Jew-
ish Church of which blood to flow was made, reminded;
and much pains he a ritual suitable to devise took. He,
the ceremony, in the vestry in case a weaker vessel or the
Bishop offended should be, to be performed, ordained;
and I, of Rudolph the heart-brother and life-friend, the
actual tattooing to do, was chosen.

Yesterday, *Gott in Himmel*, the marriage, the tattooing
including, celebrated was.

Today, of Rudolph the bride to him will not speak,
and to her mother back has gone and I, of Rudolph the
nose, in the vestry, have flattened and have punched,
because he, me of him of hearts the heart-friend and
brother, "*verfluchter Schweinhund*," called.

But I calm must be, and down the story, without
comment set.

I, to the altar, Rudolph, as best man, attended; and at
of the religious ceremony the conclusion, to the vestry
a solemn procession proceeded. First, seven little boys,
thuribles swinging, went; by the choir, hymns singing,
followed. Then six in white clothes little girls who on
the ground flowers threw; then Rudolph with on his arm
the bride, of whom the robe of satin white most glori-
ous and bloom of orange by six bridesmaids was borne.
Then an acolyth on a with gold fringe red velvet cush-
ion the tattooing instruments; a fine cork of Heidseick
Dry Monopole in which three needles stuck were, and of
Indian ink a stick, bearing. Then between two clergymen,

I, of Rudolph and his bride the brother and tattooer, and last, of the happy pair the relations and friends.

The bride and bridegroom in the vestry on two velvet chairs sat; the clergy, choir, bridesmaids and friends round the walls in a neat group themselves placed. Then Rudolph, in a silver dish, his finger at the acute angle put, and I, at it, with the three needles in the cork stuck, jabbed.

When of Rudolph the blood spurted, a bridesmaid, a noise which like "Yawps" sounded, made, and to giggle began: and my heart-brother his teeth ground and gritted; and words, which to be said ought not, said, and as often as at the finger I jabbed, and of blood the drops into the dish did roll (for Rudolph a man of full habit of body is), a fresh bridesmaid, "Yawps" saying, off to giggling went; until the whole room round and round before my eyes hum did.

Nevertheless I, a kind of ring round Rudolph's finger, made, and into it, all bloody, the Indian ink rubbed, and then to the fine rich went, the same thing to do.

But "Yawps" all the female women and the clergy now giggling, said, and Rudolph "sharp look, and with it done be," said; and the bride into the dish because of the blood in it her finger, would not put, but it out straight, held; and she, the acolyth with the dish, shook; and of the blood a drop, on of her gown the front, went; and I her finger seized; and the needles into it, jabbed; and she it away screaming, snatched; and to Rudolph that he, her, that it would hurt, had not told, said; and that of the nasty man the hands all bloody, were, said; and everybody giggling stopped, and with the bride to shriek began; and of the bride the mother, to Rudolph that he was a brute, said; and to me, Rudolph, that I *"verfluchter Schweinhund"* was, said; and I, of him the nose, with all of me the might, punched; and there some policemen were; and I, of the conclusion, a distinct recollection, have not.

But to her mother the nefifat rich of Yorkshire fräulein has returned; and Rudolph, no bride nor of her money, has; and I, Rudolph, my of all hearts the heart-friend and life-brother, have lost, and in the good of hypnotism is my faith destroyed; and therefore I, without, of the suggesting that wedding rings of men as well as women tattooed should be, maniac female, the blood, consoled cannot be.

# THE ARMED HANDS

(CIRCA 1906)

L IFE is a grotesque series of magic-lantern pictures: at least, mine is. I am among a heavily-
breathing intense mob, in the dark. Suddenly,
the Showman flashes before me a brilliant disc of a picture quite unrelated to its surroundings. It stays, during
a moment—I don't know how. It means—I can't think
what. It vanishes—I don't know where. And life is as ob-
scurely uninteresting as before—I haven't a notion why.

For example: I saw three blazingly clear pictures at
Oxford in Eights Week. I make a point of being up during Eights Week, because (as a physical epicure) I like to
see how England's most recent flesh is coming on. It (as
you know) is on view daily, at 16.30 and 18 p.m., on the
towing-path between the Osteria Iside and the barges.

On the first morning, Thursday, I went out for a daw-
dle before my coffee. I prowled, for no earthly reason,
a little way up the Via Woodstochiana. Few people are
abroad in Oxford at 7 o'clock of the morn, excepting on
the paths which lead to Il Piacere de' Parocchi. Anyhow,
Campo Sant' Egidio and that little bit of Via Woodstochiana were deserted at that particular moment. As the

first of my three pictures was exhibited in this neigh-
bourhood, it will be well to precise the spot.

On the left of the Via Woodstochiana, the shops
ended with a sort of emporium. Then, there was an alley;
and, on the other side of the alley, a fairly-sizeable plain
house. The alley seemed quite an ordinary stone-paved
little slipe. On its south side, was the side-wall of the
dwelling pertaining to the emporium. On its north side,
was the side-wall of the plain house. The front-doors of
these two buildings were not in Via Woodstochiana but
in the alley, one facing the other. In squinting up the alley,
I fancied that it led to a third (but rather more embellished) building. I hope that this is all clear.

As I turned into the alley from motives of inquisitive-
ness, I saw a man approaching me. I did not particularly
note him at the time, beyond the fact that his face wore
the positively indescribable (but saliently recognisable)
expression of one who has just prayed well. But he certainly did strike me as being as grey a man as I could wish
to see. I don't mean his hair: he was bare-headed, closely-
clipped, and slightly bald on the tonsure. And I don't
mean his face: that was tanned and healthy enough, and
quite in keeping with his slight (but rather broadbreast-
ed) figure and his quietly agile gait. But I mean his perfect
poise, and his sedate gravity, which were simply as grey
as grey can be. And I mean his clothes. They seemed a
symphony of dark-grey tones. Even his watch-chain and
key-chain and scarf-pin and sleeve-links had the dark-
grey gleam of platinum; and his neat slippers were of
dark-grey suede. The white of his collar, the white of the
silk-handkerchief in his sleeve and the black of his neck-

tie, were just what was wanted to bind his colour-scheme beautifully together. I never in my life have seen a man looking so simply and calmly staid. Indeed, after passing him,—we met midway between the embellished edifice and the two side front-doors which I have mentioned,—I could not help looking back at him. And then, without the very slightest warning, the picture was flashed upon my brain.

This was it. I was well up the alley and looking down it toward Via Woodstochiana. The Grey Man was in the alley between the door of the plain house and the door of the emporium. All of a sudden, both doors slid open inwardly and silently. A thick-set gentleman in glossy black oozed out of the plain house-door; and said something affably to the Grey Man. It seemed also to be civil: but the distance, of course, rendered it inaudible by me. It could not have been more than six words. The Grey Man, without halting, gave a courteously-negative gesture with his head. A burly red-bearded fellow slipped out of the open emporium-door; and began (with the glossy black gentleman) to butt and hustle the Grey Man toward the open door of the plain house. The Grey Man sprang, like a kitten, one pace backward; and instantly rebounded forward, launching a lightning-like right-and-left double-knock—ping-pang, pong-pung—across the two foreheads. Blood splashed out in the most extraordinary manner. I never before saw such gushings. I heard two swiftly-sucked-in breaths and a couple of stifled groans. The assailants, carrying their heads, staggered into their respective houses. The doors shut as noiselessly as they had opened. The Grey Man quite quietly went on his unruffled way.

All this happened while one could count nine. It blazed into vision for nine seconds; and, then, was not. It, indeed, was so amazing, that (for an instant) I believed myself to be the subject of an hallucination. So I stepped back to the mouth of the alley. There were puddles of fresh gore, on the pavement between the doorways. I looked out into the Via Woodstochiana. There, was the Grey Man demurely crossing Campo Sant' Egidio by the cabmen's shelter, and going in the direction of the Collegio di San Zanbatista. He went with easy swiftness, his hands in his trousers' pockets. If I had not already noticed him, I certainly should have failed to do so, so accurately did he come with the landscape.

It was excessively queer. I won't deny that I stood and pondered the event, perhaps for a couple of minutes. For the life of me I couldn't understand what I had seen. Still, it obviously was no affair of mine. I thought, however, that I might well postpone exploration of that alley and go home and have my coffee. So I did.

✳

The fourth day after that was Sunday. In the evening I dined with old Sniffles at his house on Muro Lungo. That man's collection of intagliate alexandroliths ought to fetch quite a quarter of a million when he turns up his toes. We spent the whole evening in pawing the gems.

As I mounted my bicycle at his door, at last, a clock announced the half past 23; and all the other timepieces in the city corroborated the statement. Several spoke together, very discordantly: of course there were the usual laggards: but the gist of the testimony was fairly unanimous. As it was a fine night, I resolved to ride a little way before tucking up. The dark darkness of night suits my thinking apparatus better than the light darkness of day—the fat dismal unwieldly ordinary uneventful day. So I went up Via del Santo Pozzo into Via Larga; and turned the corner, intending to ride up Via Banburiana as far as Città Destate and back. Be it always and everywhere and by everyone remembered that I had no reason whatever for this choice of route. It just occurred to me to go that way; and I as simply went.

I suppose that, if the Oxford policemen read this, they will feel bound to lay a trap and run me in. The fact is that, instead of going by road round the fore-court of Collegio di San Zanbatista, I pedalled lazily through the posts and all along the pavement in front of the old college-buildings, just like an ordinary undergraduate at 10 a.m. Not a soul breathed near. Even after I had got through the second set of posts, I did not trouble to leave the pavement immediately, but rode along the façade of the new college-buildings, passing the first lamp-post, and only gliding into the road on reaching the second before the administrator's office. And it was here that the second picture unexpectedly glared me in the face.

You understand that I had the Uffiizio Amministrativo del Collegio di San Zanbatista on my right hand, and was about to pass the adjoining entry which leads to the college. Beyond this entry was a new-faced Casa Iacopesca joined to a pub which (in turn) attached itself to the row of houses before you come to the Allogio dei Giudici. On my left, stretched the great dim open width and length of Campo Sant' Egidio with its leafy avenues. Before me, the pavement lay like a grey ribbon. There was a fair light on the foreground of it, a light shed by a third lamp-post which stood at the juncture of the Casa Iacopesca and the pub: but, beyond that, the middle distance faded gradually into the night.

Just when I was crawling by the Uffizio Amministrativo of the college, I recognized the Grey Man. He came toward me from the direction of Via Banburiana; and I spotted him as he came into the light of the third lamp-post. Quite instantaneously the double door of the Casa Iacopesca opened like a dumb mouth. Two small ghostly gentlemen pranced out. They both sported black trousers and peculiarly long black jackets agreeably slit up the rear. One was long-bodied and stumpy-legged: the other was grotesquely verdant-greeny: both wore snubbed noses and spectacles. And they, also, set themselves silently to butt and hustle the Grey Man into the blackness of their open door. Then followed the same two hideous crashes of fists upon foreheads, the same two spouting sheets of blood, the same suppressed squeals and unhesitating evanishments, the same slammed speechless door, and the same impassive invulnerable solitary figure pursuing its mysterious way.

Mind you—this time, I was not a couple of yards distant from the collision. The whole thing was begun and finished by the time I had pedalled four times. Nothing could have been smarter. I had not even time to dismount—much less to say something equivalent to 'Ciò!'

I gazed at the Casa Iacopesca. All the windows were blind. There was a glimmer in the bar of the pub beyond: but not a movement anywhere. I looked all round. No one was in sight, excepting the moth-grey figure passing through the posts of San Zanbatista. I very much wanted to run after him. But of course that was out of the question.

And, then, you must know something else. I really was seized (at the moment) with grave doubt concerning my quality of visibility. None of these gladiators seemed to have noticed me at all. They popped out, and did their trick, and scuttled back into their burrow (so to speak), just as though they were quite alone. It was most puzzling, not to say annoying.

The only things which I could think of, to say, in this emergency were "Mariavergine!" and "Ostreghette!" I said them alternately to myself half-a-dozen times, observing uncanonical intervals, as I rode up Via Banburiana toward Città Destate; and derived immense relief. Furthermore, just by the Giardini di Norham, a motorcar blasphemed me for riding on the wrong side of the road. This was a vast consolation: for it certified me that I could still be seen.

Some people cannot look at pictures without worrying themselves about the artist's meaning, and rot of that sort. (They are the kind of people who begin their criticisms with the formula "Ow! I down't lyke the fyce.") Now I always try to look at pictures with a sole purpose of taking my pleasure. But, I admit that the two last exhibitions tried me severely. It was irritating to feel, on the inaccessible back of one's mind, the nipping flea of curiosity. However, I just blundered on toward my grave, through my normal state of mist, till the following Wednesday.

✳

It was the last day of the Eights. The afternoon had been muggy, dully threatening rain. At 17.30 p.m. I took advantage of the interval between the two races to stroll down the towing-path. My idea was to find a place where I might observe the men—not the crews, but the men who run along the bank. I am not aware of any spot on this planet, excepting Venice, which offers a more exhaustive and instructive exhibition of vigorous physique, than this particular bit of Oxford at this particular moment. The show comprises several hundred specimens; and I solemnly aver that one in twenty is quite worth looking at twice. Why not? *Athletam in ingenuum nasci tam facile est quam accedere huc.*

The point, of getting below Ponti Lunghi for the purpose, is this. Shortly before 18 o'clock, the men come down, from the barges and elsewhere, to (say) the Osteria Iside whereby the boats are moored. When the starting-gun fires, they run back (along the towing-path) by the sides of their respective boats. To stand on the towing-path during the process, amounts to competing for being bunted (by roaring gladiators) into a fussy river. But, just below the Ponti Lunghi, the towing-path winds round the Budello; and there is a short cut across the grass from Ponti Lunghi to the point where the path follows the straightened course of the river. And it is possible

78

to preserve one's equilibrium on this grass, while taking leisured observations of the turmoil of the towing-path close by.

So, I strolled down quite early, intending to study the human current coming and going. I was rather too early. There were but few people about as yet. Punts and steamers and motor-boats were edging-in backward: and there were the usual clots of screeching little boys messing about the river-brink. Now and then, a racing-crew paddled (or bucketed) down to its station. But athletes occurred only in scanty sprinklings. I walked on to the end of the grass.

Suddenly, men began to swarm down in crowds. I turned back; and made for the unoccupied middle of the grass-patch. There was quite a lot of flesh on view, not (perhaps) of the quality of ten years ago, when the okhlotesacy had not yet been permitted to forget its place, and before the *Dylymyle* had made the nation a chronic self-conscious hysteric. But still it was by no means sickening; and, here and there, Nature proved that she had not entirely lost the knack of modelling shrines for character.

The gun went off; and the race began. Up came the crowd again, firing revolvers, whirling plangent wooden rattles, bellowing through mastodonic megaphones. As I had been moving slowly toward Ponti Lunghi to see the faces of the gymnasts going down, I was now sauntering back toward Iffleja to see them coming up. In a few minutes they had passed me, and were rampaging far up stream, leaving me almost alone again. I did not turn to follow, knowing jolly well what a block there would be on the towing-path above the boat-house, and the utter impossibility of crossing to the Prato della Casa di Cristo till all the boats had reached their proper barges, and the perennial puntful of performers had been tipped-over for the diversion of the leek-shaped virgins who concealed their right eyes with tubs made of the pelts of sea-green lions decorated with the residuum of a massacre of condors and albatrosses on the barge-tops.

I hope it is quite plain that I was not really seeing all these things which I describe—seeing them (I mean,) not with the two common or filmy eyes with which we keep our pipes alight and wink at the auctioneers and use for not avoiding temptation, but with that third transcendental esoteric clear-seeing eye hidden in the brain which gives the only vision worth while. Of course I saw the moving show, as heaps of other people saw it, as something all-of-a-sudden fuskily epileptic in a fog, something ephemeral, essentially irreproducible, obliterated utterly, gone and done with. But I don't call that Seeing, simply because it is not Hearing.

But, when I came to the end of the grass, and stepped on to the towing-path, that third eye of mine promptly etched the last of my three pictures on my mind. Coming toward me from Iffleja and about fifty yards away, was the slight Grey Man. It was a clear vision of him, face to face, which I set myself intensely to study.

I find it nearly impossible to interpret his personality in words: it was so vivid, so serene, so supremely noncurant, so exclusively aloof and distinct from every other living thing on this orb of earth. This time, he was in white, bare-legged, bare-headed. His white jacket and socks were patterned with a fine grey line: but his shorts and his zephyr were plain. His shoes and belt were of grey suede. A dark-grey chain, slipped through the jacket buttonhole, held a watch in the left breast pocket. His key-chain and belt-buckle were of the same dull-gleaming platinum-coloured metal. A white silk-handkerchief hid in his left sleeve, round which a towel was twisted; and the last item (taken in conjunction with the quality of his skin and the direction of his approach) led me to conceive that he had been swimming all by himself in the Cataratta di Guadodisabbia. There was not a single discord—there was not even a harsh or feeble note, about him anywhere. He was noticeable simply and solely because he was so exquisitely simple and sole—so singularly and so pellucidly complete in himself, and apart. I suppose that he was about five feet seven inches high; and I surmised that he would strip at about ten stone. Whoever made him, evidently understood the business: but I suspect that he himself had a hand in the job.

In judging a work of this sort, I always try to avoid the vulgar mobile's error of over-estimating details. Of course, I note them, carefully, but only as the components of a unity. The well-shaped capable feet, the well-turned legs, the supple knees, the lithe reins, the generous breast, the delightful arms and shoulder and neck, the lively uniform tan of silky skin, were (I could see in a flash) the reason, the *causa causans*, the integral elements, of this perfectly-poised personality. His gait (which, as the Preacher says, shews what a man is,) was truly marvelous in the strength and delicacy of its inevitably inerrant equilibrium. Have you ever seen one of those slim young

Nipponese acrobats pacing an almost invisible wire stretched over abysmal precipices? That was the mien of the Grey Man. Only, I was sensible that he went in no danger of falling and that he could keep up eternally. *Ostreghete!* How consummately artistic it was!

[I fear that I am keeping you waiting. My excuse is the cumbrous inadequacy of language to describe what I saw while I strolled perhaps ten steps forward.]

As he came nearer and nearer, I looked for his individuality in his face. It was a pale smooth oval face, tanned to the colour of honey. It had the very high broad brow of a student and thinker, crowned by short hair of a reddish chestnut slightly silvered. The nose was daring—straight, with sensitive nostrils. The mouth also was straight—thin and firm and recondite as to the upper lip, with a tinge of gentle tenderness lurking in the slightly fuller modelling of the lower. The eyes were dark-brown and rather long, limpidly bright in the pupils, and the white of a most wonderfully pure candour. A platinum-stepped monocle belonged in the left one. The eyebrows were darker brown, authoritatively drawn across the brow from temple to temple. The chin was the chin of a jesuitical machiavellian autocrat, like (say) Caesar Augustus, cloven and fine and compact. As for the expression—I hardly know what to say. It was the most amazingly distinct and unapproachable thing which I have yet seen. There was vivid serenity, gentleness and ruthless ferocity, quiet fastidious disdain, immense knowledge of good and of evil, fancy, wistfulness, extreme sensibility and ineffable indifference, indomitable tenacity, reserve, courage, enormous and inexhaustible force, all deliberately matured and mastered and governed by grave simple self-control. In short, it was the face of a man who has attained what Aristoteles quite luminously (and quite untranslateably) calls the *Kyria Arete*.

When he was about twenty paces away from me, his hands came out of his pockets, producing a tiny tobacco-pouch and a book of huge papers; and he began to roll a cigarette. They were well-formed hands, strong and brown and fine. There was a corn on the inner top joint of the right middle finger, caused (no doubt) by the habitual use of a pen. There were corns, also, on both thumb-joints, caused (no doubt) by use of the oar of a gondola—which was most strange, you know. And, finally, the hands were armed—there is no other suitable verb—armed, with four monstrous platinum-coloured rings.

He passed on my left; and so I could not quite make out the ring which was farthest away from me, on the third finger of his right hand. I only saw that it was a most massive band with a highly-projecting bezel in which a stone of sorts sparkled clearly from behind a grating. On his right first finger, however, was another rather-larger ring, the bezel of which seemed to be a section of a triangular cylinder pivoted to the points of a horse-shoe-shaped hoof. The base of the triangle clung to the finger: but its knife-edged apex projected outward; and the two visible sides appeared to be intagliate with inscriptions. It was the third and fourth fingers of the left hand which were similarly armed. This hand, of course, was quite near me; and I had no difficulty in making my inspection. The ring on the third finger had an oblong horizontal bezel quite an inch long: it was a signet, intagliate with what looked like an Eros Crucified. But the ring on the fourth finger was perhaps the most appallingly ferocious of the four. It was a plain heavy circle; and the bezel was the sharp-pointed revolving rowel of a spur.

When I say that none of these rings projected less than a quarter-of-an-inch anywhere, while the prominent portions of them jutted out a good half-inch from the fingers, you will realise what terrifically trenchant weapons they really were. Given freedom, close-quarters, physical force and skill and promptitude behind them, and their cusped spines and sharp edges and snaggy corners and blunt weight furnished a complete apparatus for inflicting the whole gamut of (not necessarily mortal) mutilations, from bruising and scratching to gashing and slicing.

And that is all.

We passed each other on the towing-path, the incarnate enigma going toward Ponti Lunghi, while I blundered on toward the Osteria Iside for a much-needed drink. And that is all. I don't know who the Grey Man is, or why extreme measures are used to secure his company, or why he punches and gashes people and blinds them with their blood on sight, or anything at all about him beyond what I have told you. And, on the whole, I don't think that I want to know any more. I have received three sharp and violently interesting impressions, I would rather not see them worked up and coloured. They are perfectly satisfactory to me in outline.

※

[By the bye, lest I should be deemed guilty of the habit of staring, let me hasten to explain, first, that I carefully cultivate my senses of seeing and differentiating and selecting to help me in my mystery of painting, and, second, that (when out to observe) I wear black glasses and keep my head still to prevent objects from knowing how they are regarded.]

# THE PRINCESS'S SHIRTS

(MAY 1906)

THE old Princess of Cinthyanum sometimes gave reasons for her indignant intolerance of political clergymen, especially Jesuits. She had no patience with people who set up to be Arbiters of both spiritual and temporal Elegancies. When she was in this mood she was extremely interesting.

"Tell me, Princess," said Nicholas Crabbe, "did they ever hurt you personally?" Tea was just over. It was a summer afternoon, in the gardens of the palace among the Alban Hills. The Princess was gazing dreamily over the placid lake of Nemi.

"Come indoors; and I'll answer you," she briefly replied.

As they ascended the terrace steps, the gardener's son, Toto, came through the hydrangea bushes with his violin. Seeing Her Excellency, he stopped, and began to play. He was a marvellous *improvisatore*. The old lady and her guest went into the boudoir; and sat in silence, listening to the lovely passionate music.

Toto's fiddle spat a spiteful syncopated *pizzicato*; and burst off into silence. The two souls, in the cool shady room above him, took a fresh lease of their tongues.

"Did they ever hurt me personally?" the Princess began. "Why, even now I boil with rage when I think of the time when they used to hurt me every day. Did they ever, indeed! Tell me what you think of this. I permit you to smoke. It was in 1866. The matches are behind you. My darling Prince had just exceeded human things. Francesco and Bosio were fighting with the King in the north. I was alone in my widowhood, here, through the winter. It was an awful winter. The Garibaldian army was down there in the ravine beneath my window. I'll get you an ash-tray. On the other side of the palace, about a mile along the road to Rome, Bomba of Naples was encamped, with the troops which he had brought to help Pio Nono. Both armies were waiting for the frost to break.

"The Garibaldians were adventurers—brigands. I detested them, although they did happen to be on the right side. Beside, what sort of a person was Garibaldi, I should like to know? How your English duchesses could pet a man like that in their drawing-rooms, is a mystery to me. I wouldn't have had such riffraff in my courtyard. They had no commissariat whatever. Madonna alone knows how they contrived to live.

"One morning, I heard my maids saying that thirteen of the rascals had been frozen to death during the night. I made inquiries. Every night of frost had killed from ten to twenty of them. Actually they didn't dare to touch a stick of my woods. Horrid, wasn't it? The city was talking. You don't suppose I was going to permit that. Luckily, I've always kept a good stock of flannels and blankets here, to give to my poor. I hadn't been in Cinthyanum the four previous winters; and so I had four years' stocks accumulated here in 1866. Touch that bell, please. So I sent all my blankets down to the Garibaldians at once. An apron, Birnie—the one with the bugles—and a handkerchief, Birnie, please. Then I got all the women of the city who would sew for a wage, a hundred and nineteen of them; and I spread them in long lines in the picture-gallery; and I and my maids cut the flannel into shirts; and the women sewed them; and, as fast as they were finished, I sent them down to the Garibaldians.

"Toto's father's brother was a nimble lad of sixteen then. He was called Toto too. And he used to do the risky job of climbing down the rock with my bundles every night. This went on for nearly a fortnight. Bomba's Neapolitans got to hear of it; and shot at him several times. They were abominable marksmen. He was as quick and limber as a kitten, and quite fearless. He used to laugh about it.

"At last, though, they caught him—the brave boy—and killed him. Don't take any notice of me. Go and look out of that window for a minute. You see the little ruined tower, on the crag, just across the ravine? Well, they stripped him naked, and walled him up there, not a hundred yards from where you're standing. What a night we had, when he didn't come back! The next day I turned the city out to search for him. We found him at avemmaria, quite dead—frozen stiff. His eyes were open; he was standing, leaning against the wall, looking this way through that broken window. How black his hair was against the snow! I can't think why I'm crying. I am so proud of him. It was such a grand death to die. One of my dear darling Italy's noble army of martyrs.

"You remember that Venetian who did the bronze, called 'Intervallo,' of a lad on a rock flipping the ash from a cigarette. He was staying with some friends of his here, just then; and he saw it all. What an old fool I am, to be sure! But oh, my dear Crabbe, when they brought that white thing for me to see, it was just like a marble god: the plump proud agile voluptuous face and form, the opulent young flesh, the splendid great long plain curving contours. Urbane Bottasso said he'd never seen anything like it, except when he dreamed about Hermes. But you know the image. Signor Urbane did it for me afterwards, to stand on the altar which I put over there. Arrow? Yes, we gave him an arrow to make him a saint. Sebastian, you know. He died all alone, too. But that's exactly how Toto looked. I had him buried standing, just as he was. There, I'm better now.

"The same afternoon a file of paparchal dragoons brought me an order to cross the frontier within six hours, on pain of force. I told the lieutenant that I didn't dispute Pio Nono's right as my sovereign to send me into perpetual exile: but I thought that I, as a Roman patrician, had a right to know my crime, even though I was to be punished without trial.

"'Her Excellency has been in treasonable communication with the enemy,' says he.

"'I've clothed the naked, if His Holiness calls that treason,' says I.

"'But, Excellency, *the shirts were red!*' says he.

"I'm bound to say I laughed. Of course they were! Tell me, did you ever hear of an Englishwoman who kept any flannel but red by her for the poor? But that was the first thought which I'd given to it. Till that moment, I protest to you, the idea had never entered my head that I'd been making red shirts—uniforms, in fact—for those rascally Garibaldians. Of course I was a traitress. And not a bit ashamed. Rather proud, in fact.

"So I packed up and went to London, and took a house in Granville Place.

"Now here's somebody coming to call. No: I've not done yet. You shall hear the rest after dinner. Did they ever hurt me personally, indeed!"

# DEINON TO THELY

(JANUARY 1909)

THE Princess of Cinthyanum pushed her dessert-plate, opining that life was too short for eating prickly-pears.

"I think they're the most delicious fruit in the world. I'm sure they're what the angels eat in Heaven. But do consider the form they take here—little tiny parcels of what's purely ambrosia, each packed separately in the crevices of a huge core made of sharp steel knife-blades. No doubt there's a moral lesson in it. I suppose it's meant to teach us that nothing really nice is to be had without no end of pains. Every time I see a prickly pear, I feel perfectly piggish. I'd suck them, if the cores didn't gash my palate into slices. Do you know what I want? I want a clean slave, with very dainty fingers and a little silver scoop, who would sit by me all through dinner, and pick me out a plateful of prickly-pear pulp, so that I might eat it for dessert with a table-spoon. But there—we never get what we want."

"No," said Nicholas Crabbe.

"Why do you say 'No' like that? Are you nourishing a secret yearning too?"

"I am," he answered. "You began to tell me a lovely tale about the way in which what you call the Arbiters-of-temporal-as-well-as-spiritual-Elegancies hurt you personally. It was a truly ripping tale; but there was nothing about Arbiters in it, as far as you went. Then, that horrible brown marchioness with fat stockings came to call, and interrupted you; and you promised to tell me the rest after dinner. It is after dinner now."

"Let's have coffee first. Three lumps or four? Can't understand that I don't talk about those dreadful Arbiters, just simply because I talk of nothing else. They aren't in my stories: they're the story itself."

"How?"

"Why, because they're at the back of them all. Look here: you know that I am friendly with the Order of Divine Love. I knew its founder. A saint, he was; and thought quite properly about the king too. Well then; the Arbiters don't think properly about the king; and so they're the enemies of the Divine Lovers, just as the Dominicans used to be of the Franciscans, on account of some trumpery politics."

Nicholas shook his head with a gesture despairing of unraveling these intricacies.

"I know," he said, "that the Order of Divine Love is under a cloud just now: because of some thirty-nine propositions, which Leo the Thirteenth commodiously anathematized a little while ago."

The Princess put her hands in her apron pockets, and set out to be categorical.

"I'll have you know," she asserted, "that those propositions were not theological, but philosophical."

"What difference does that make?"

"The difference that they're profoundly unimportant. Everyone knows how absurdly philosophers philosophise on such subjects as (for example) the unanswerable question as to the number of angels who can dance on the point of a needle. No one dreams of cursing pious old maids of the masculine gender, who waste their time in arguing that the moon either is, or is not, made of green cheese, and that, as it certainly is not, therefore it is. These diverting pastimes are comparatively harmless. The thirty-nine damned propositions are, as I thought all the world knew, simply a subterfuge. The real reason why the Order of Divine Love is in Rome's black book is something quite different. Leo the Thirteenth is all very well: but what I'm talking about happened under Pius the Ninth. I've known three paparchs personally—Gregory, Pius, and Leo—and every one of them has been the tool, or mouthpiece, or catspaw, of some monkey in the background. When Domeniddio gave us Pio Nono, I remember thinking that we'd gotten a Man with a mind of His own. He'd been about a bit, you know. But he turned out as They all do, only much worse. Oh yes; well-meaning, of course, and all that kind of thing; but never able to make a plan and stick to it; and always under someone's thumb. First, it was one; then the other; after that, the next; and never the same for a year together. Well, and so in the revolutionary days, He came under the influence of Father Antonino Rosmarini, who founded my dear Order of Divine Love. That was the best thing which could possibly happen to His Holiness. Rosmarini, you must know, was a rather fantastic broad-churchman, a real idealist, for (as you say) the Ideal is the Real, seen as it is. He contrived to persuade Pio Nono to become poor, and without possessions, and so to be the lord and sovereign of all things. Isn't that pretty? In fact, Rosmarini was employed to compile the Bull which was to proclaim this new arrangement. Pio Nono was so much in love with his notions, that He denounced him cardinal *in petto*. How do I know? Why, because Rosmarini had his state-chariot built, with his armorials blazoned on the panels; and we stored it in our coach-house in Rome till he could use it. But the Arbiters didn't like this poverty-business at all. Their philosophy, you know, prefers being poor with great possessions. So they scampered in, and began to argue against Rosmarini with all their might. A pack of diorthòtic pedants, I call them, with a mania for setting people right. The Paparch wavered: being one of those amiable ineptitudes who feel pained when their children scuffle. And then, Rosmarini very intempestively died, leaving behind him the draft of the Apostolic Bull, and his newly-pledged Order of Divine Love, and his state-chariot in our stable. The Arbiters, of course, came into power as paparchal advisers: because no one else had the policy cut and dried at the moment. They promptly used the draft of Rosmarini's bull for pipe-lights and other purposes. They bade the Divinie Lovers to stand in the corner, till such time when their founder's writings could be examined and corrected. And I'll tell you what became of the chariot another time. The Arbiters took twenty years or so, as you see, over the second job. Rosmarinis apostolic views, concerning the trivial question of Temporal Power, were considered to infect his spiritual sons.

But the Order of Divine Love hasn't been damned on that count; because the world would have laughed all over its newspapers. Instead the Arbiters (like the sage serpents they are) waited till Pio Nono had evolated to the superiors, and till they'd made their own position secure as Leo's directors; and then, those thirty-nine harmless intensely uninteresting and altogether negligible propositions were picked out of Rosmarini's philosophy, and ceremonially cursed, as you say. Don't pay the slightest attention to it. The sheep of Christ's flock are always being neglected, while the shepherds exchange anathemas. That's one of the many comical ways in which Christians love one another. It's not one of the things that matter. So make your mind easy. Of course, I'm glad to see my friends, the Divine Lovers, have incontinently submitted, and thrown the thirty-nine propositions overboard. And now they've quietly retired into private life, like the sensible saints they are, until the tyranny of those oligarchic Arbiters shall be overpast. My dear Crabbe, you know it's a frightful waste of time to kick against the pricks."

"Well?" said Nicholas, undesirous of sermons and personalities.

"That's all," the Princess starkly announced.

"All about the Divine Lovers, perhaps; but you were going to tell me how the Arbiters hurt you personally."

"God, bless this man! Haven't I been telling you about it all this time?"

"Only by faint indirections. I suppose you mean that the Arbiters were behind Pius the Ninth when he banished you—"

"I do. And then think of the way they made Him treat me when my darling Bosio was married. Oh, my dear Crabbe, you don't know half—"

"But I'm sitting here, dying—simply dying, Princess—to (ha!) well, to know all."

"You're not smoking! Well, I do call that a compliment. Have you got cigarettes? Do smoke one here. Are you sure my gossip doesn't bore you? Where did I leave off when the Ascapettatoli came?"

"You went to spend your exile in England."

"So I did. And took a house in Granville Place. Yes. And then my poor dear Bosio must needs get married. You see what Valeria is now? You'd never have thought she'd turn out so splendidly, if you'd seen her then. She was a gaunt, long-legged white-skinned hoyden of fifteen on her wedding-day, without a single good feature to her name, except her hair. Madonnina, what hair it was! It was the palest, brightest yellow I ever saw; and she really and truly could cover herself with it from head to foot, just like Diva Agnes. We think a lot of those sparkling flaxen girls in Italy; because they're so rare, you know. It was an excellent match in every way. The County of Santa Cotogna is a very good title. Though it is only our second, it's older than all our duchies and princedoms. In fact, till only the other day, it was a sovereign tyranny, with a knighthood of the Golden Quince, and rights of the pit, gibbet, and the question, all complete. So I can promise you that my poor Bosio was extremely respectable. Valeria, of course, was a Poplicola in her own right; and I don't need to tell you what that means. It was an immense relief to me to hear that they fancied each other. My darling Bosio was a great anxiety to me. One never quite knew but what some day he might give one for a daughter—but that doesn't signify. Well; they arranged to be married at Turin. Of course, I wanted to be present. But to get to Turin, in those days, from England, meant going through a bit of what were then the Paparchal States. And I happened to be a bandit, liable to arrest on sight. Monsignor Ermogene, the dear, arranged that difficulty for me; and the Holy Father was persuaded not to be a beast, and prevent a mother from seeing her son married. What harm could an old woman like me do, just by driving across His Holiness's territories and back; for that was all the indulgence permitted. So I went to Turin, and saw them safely married. Lord, how pretty they were! Then, it appeared that Valeria was determined to spend her honeymoon at a castle of hers at Deira, right down in the south by Reggio. She was a most wilful young woman, even then. Nothing would put her off it. The Poplicolae, of course, came from Ardea originally; but I forget which paparch took that place away from them and gave it to us. It doesn't matter; because it happened quite four hundred years ago. But, you see, Deira, consequently, is the oldest place they have left. She had a little sentiment about it. There she'd go; and nowhere else. But what was the use of her going alone? Who ever heard of such a thing as a girl leaving her husband at the altar-steps for the sake of a sentiment about a tower? Dear me! I suppose I've left something out—"

"Why couldn't her husband go with her?"

"Yes, that's it. You see, my poor dear Bosio was a bandit as well as his wretched mother. Don't dare to think that it runs in the family. Nothing of the kind. I'm proud to say that I'm the only deliberate criminal of the Attendoli-Cesari in this century. My darling Bosio wasn't a bit to blame. It was forced on him. He did so many noble deeds all through the war that the king gave him the medal For Valour on the battlefield, and the Romans elected him senator. He couldn't help being elected, could he? But that's why Pio Nono put the ban upon him—at the insistence of the Arbiters, I needn't say. Well; there we were, planted at Turin; Valeria swearing that she would go to Deira, which meant quite a long journey through the Paparchal States; me, a bandit; and Bosio, in the same plight. He was quite willing to risk arrest, and capital sentence, and all the other unpleasantnesses which those rascals had ready for him. Can't I imagine how they'd have glutted themselves with the head of a Roman patrician! They didn't often get a chance of making an example of a man of my Bosio's consequence. He said that he could get through secretly. I really believe he thought an adventure like that would be rather a lark. Men are so queer. But I and Valeria both shrieked at him, till he promised not to be rash. Besides, supposing he had put on a false nose, or something of that kind; and suppose he had managed to evade the Arbiters and their informers, who simply infested the whole peninsula; what good would that have been? Deira is in what was then the kingdom of Naples; and the King of Naples was Pio Nono's ally. It wasn't a question of flitting by night through an enemy's country. It was simply going straight into the depths of it, and thinking oneself safe there. What that girl really wanted was a plenary indulgence for her husband to spend his honeymoon in Pio's friend's kingdom, and a safe-conduct there and back. Neither more, nor less. To my mind, she might just as well have wanted the morning-star. However, I myself had to go on to Rome, to pay my respects to and to thank my sovereign for His clemency in letting me come to my son's marriage; and I said I'd see if anything could be done. Off I went. The Holy Father was receiving ambassadors; but I claimed my privilege as Roman patrician, and saw them all shunted into an antechamber, while I sailed straight into The Presence. Pio let me go down on my knees—didn't say a single word, and never even offered me a stool. Why, He wouldn't even concede my patrician's right to His hand—just stuck out His foot, as though I were Mrs Anybody. Horrid of Him, wasn't it? I was younger then than I am now; but not by any means what you'd call a young woman. Bless me, how hard that floor was! And there was His Holiness sitting stiff and as black as night. People used to rave about His good looks. As for me, I don't think I ever saw a more repulsive face. Nothing is so ugly as a good weak man trying to look hard and bad. All the same, I didn't forget what I'd come for. I behaved very humbly—the hypocrite that I was!— recited my little piece, you know—told Him how grieved I was to have offended Him, how grateful I was for His kindness, and would He be so good as to make a mother happy by letting her son have a pleasant honeymoon. What do you think His answer was? Nothing at all. He got off His throne without a word, and waddled away, leaving me rooted where I was. My dear Crabbe, you know, I've the greatest possible respect for the Holy

Father, and all that kind of thing, but you must admit that no gentleman ever would have behaved like that to a lady. Well, I managed to pick up my old bones, and toddled back to Turin. 'My dears,' says I, 'it's no good. The Holy Father's a bit of a bounder. He won't even speak to me.' And I told them how elaborately I'd been humiliated. Bosio was furious. As for Valeria—well, you know her well enough to understand how she went on. 'You stay here and console your mother,' says she to Bosio, 'and I'll go and have a try. I'm by way of being a Roman patrician myself,' says she; 'and I'd like to see any man, paparch or pork-butcher, who'll dare to deny me a thing I've set my heart upon.' Pretty bold for a girl of fifteen just out of her convent, wasn't it? So off she swam. When she entered The Presence, Pio Nono seems to have been in a better humour. He found her *simpatica*, and ordered a stool for her at once. Dear me, what a difference those few days of marriage had made to her— especially her neck. You know, quite the loveliest thing in the world is a slim girl who has been happily married for a week or two. I expect she looked something amazing in her black lace, and her heavenly hair piled up and crowned with the Poplicola cat's-eyes. Have you seen that crown? It's the most wonderful thing. Fourteen enormous balls as big as five-shilling pieces—green, you know, and with the mysterious lambent light always moving round to look at you. I always say that it makes her head look as though it were full of huge eyes. She shall show it to you some day. Well; there they sat, all happy and comfortable, He on His throne, and she on her stool paying Him all kinds of pretty compliments, and cooing like the dove she never was. And presently she began to wheedle Him. 'Ah, Santissimo,' says she, 'but what an unhappy girl am I!' 'And why, pray?' says the Holy Father. 'What else can I be, when You're so unkind?' says she. Pio Nono stared. He didn't understand that at all. 'There's my poor husband in Turin, dying to pay his respects to You, and You want to cut off his head,' says she. 'Ah,'' says He, 'but what a naughty girl, to go and marry into such a family—a most dangerous family, the General Arbiter says, and with such a mother-in-law, too!' Rude of Him, wasn't it? 'Ah, well, Holy Father,' says Valeria, 'I didn't marry my mother-in-law; but she really is Your best friend, if You'll believe me,' says she, 'and how can I spend my honeymoon at Deira, unless You'll be a dear and let my husband take me there?' says she. 'Certainly not,' snaps the Paparch, short and sharp. Valeria bursts out crying at once. That made Him uncomfortable. 'Oh, what will people think of me?' says she. 'Fancy a young married woman gadding about like this without her husband! It's not respectable,' says she, leaning her cheek against His knee. 'There, there,' says He, to console her; 'but, you know, you should have thought about that before you married the man,' says He. 'Ah well, Holy Father, it's done now and can't be undone,' says she. And, without letting Pio Nono see what she was doing, she began to fumble under he veil for the pins which held her crown on. 'That's true,' says He, puzzling in a quandary. 'Then we must make the best of it,' says she. 'Yes,' says He, 'you'd better go back and try to make the best of it,' says He. 'I'm not going back without what I came for,' says Valeria. 'And that is?' 'Your Holiness's safe-conduct and plenary indulgence for my darling husband.' 'No,' says Pio. 'Yes,' says Valeria, shouting. And then, my dear Crabbe, all in a moment, she flung herself on her knees, tore off her crown and slipped her arm through it; all her lovely hair fell down in floods, and covered her and the throne-steps and everything. And then she caught His hand in both of hers, and swore that she'd never let it go till He gave her what she wanted. It's a solemn fact. Did He? Of course He did, after a bit—walked over to a table, with her hanging on His hand, and wrote the whole thing out then and there. And what's more, she declares that He actually helped her to twist up her hair and put her crown on again, in case the curia should have cause for *admiratio*. She says she never laughed so much in her life. And now I think that's all. She came back to Turin, and I saw them both off for Deira. Then I went back to my exile in England, where I stayed till Vittorio Emmanuele, who may have been a beast, but who certainly was a gentleman, was master of Rome."

"Thanks," says Nicholas. "But, Princess, didn't you ever make it up with Pius the Ninth?"

"Never. They wouldn't let Him make it up with me."

"And that's why you dislike them?"

"It is."

"I think I understand," said Nicholas Crabbe.